F

HIGH STAKES

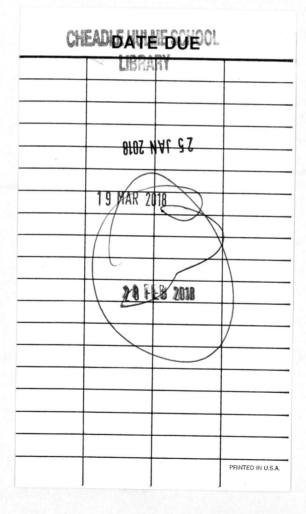

Other books by Maggie Dana

Kate and Holly: The Beginning (Timber Ridge Riders)
Keeping Secrets, Timber Ridge Riders (Book 1)
Racing into Trouble, Timber Ridge Riders (Book 2)
Riding for the Stars, Timber Ridge Riders (Book 3)
Wish Upon a Horse, Timber Ridge Riders (Book 4)
Chasing Dreams, Timber Ridge Riders (Book 5)
Almost Perfect, Timber Ridge Riders (Book 6)
Taking Chances, Timber Ridge Riders (Book 7)
After the Storm, Timber Ridge Riders (Book 8)
Double Feature, Timber Ridge Riders (Book 9)
Flying Changes, Timber Ridge Riders (Book 10)
Horse Camp, Timber Ridge Riders (Book 11)
Something Royal, Timber Ridge Riders (Book 12)
High Stakes, Timber Ridge Riders (Book 13)

Turning on a Dime ~ a time travel adventure
The Golden Horse of Willow Farm, Weekly Reader Books
Remember the Moonlight, Weekly Reader Books
Best Friends series, Troll Books/Scholastic

Sign up for our mailing list and be among the first to know when
the next Timber Ridge Riders book will be out.
Send your email address to:
timberridgeriders@gmail.com

For more information about the series, visit:
www.timberridgeriders.com
Note: all email addresses are kept strictly confidential.

TIMBER RIDGE RIDERS
Book 13

HIGH STAKES

Maggie Dana

PAGEWORKS PRESS

ISBN 978-0-9909498-4-8

Published by Pageworks Press
Text set in Sabon

for Smokey and Webster,
the best first ponies in the world

1

KATE MCGREGOR KICKED OFF both stirrups, flexed her ankles, and gave a contented sigh. Life didn't get much better than this—she and her brand new sister riding through the woods on their favorite horses. And, best of all, they were alone—no Princess Twiggy tagging along.

"Hey, what's that, down there?" Kate said, pointing toward a wide gap in the trees that hadn't been there the last time they'd ridden this way.

Holly Chapman shrugged. "A new trail?"

"I guess," Kate said.

But this wasn't a trail. It looked like an old dirt road that had been recently cleared. Its rutted tracks hinted at earthmoving equipment. On both sides of the road were mounds of fresh earth sprouting weeds.

Was Mrs. Dean up to more skullduggery?

The previous month, she'd almost trashed Timber Ridge with her plans for a tacky theme park that nobody wanted, not even the younger kids. But this trail was miles away from the barn, on the other side of the mountain and far beyond Mrs. Dean's reach.

"Looks interesting," Holly said.

"Let's check it out." Kate reconnected with her stirrups and looked at the dirt road again. It sloped downward in a perfect S bend, curving gently around half-buried rock walls and broken fencing.

Partway down the hill was a faded red barn with lopsided doors, peeling paint, and roof shingles that curled up like stale bread. On the peak, a rusty weathervane tilted crazily to one side. Beyond it, Kate saw a vine-covered farmhouse and overgrown meadows dotted with yellow daisies. There was even a small wooden bridge over a burbling stream. In the distance, a white church steeple pierced the vivid blue sky.

Picture-postcard Vermont.

A couple of months from now, this trail would be crowded with leaf-peeping tourists; in winter, skiers would carve graceful turns through drifts of deep snow.

But right now, it was a mystery.

Kate had lived at Timber Ridge for just over a year and didn't know the mountain as well as Holly, who'd lived here all her life. So why didn't she know about this farm?

"Haven't you seen it before?" Kate said.

"Duh-uh," Holly said. "I was in a wheelchair, remember?"

"Oh, sorry," Kate replied.

Looking at Holly now, with both legs wrapped firmly around Magician, it was hard for Kate to remember that her stepsister had once been paralyzed and unable to walk or ride.

Something caught Kate's eye.

She rode closer. An oval sign, suspended between two wooden fence posts, swung in the breeze. Unlike the dilapidated barn, the sign was bright and shiny and new, almost as if the paint hadn't yet dried.

Behind her, Holly said, "What does it say?"

"*Weathervane Farm*," Kate replied.

"That's all?"

"No, there's more." Kate scrunched up her eyes. In letters too small to read unless you were right on top of them were the words, *Sam Callahan, Trainer*.

"Sam Callahan?" Holly said.

To make sure, Kate read the sign again. "Yup."

But it didn't make sense. What was a big-name trainer doing in the middle of Vermont, miles away from anywhere? Sam Callahan had trained Olympic riders, and he wrote articles for *The Chronicle of the Horse*. His son, Luke, was drop-dead gorgeous.

A blush crept up Kate's face.

This always happened when she thought about boys

and about Luke Callahan in particular. Last month, he'd admired Tapestry at the end-of-camp horse show—enough to make a girl swoon. Kate's blush deepened, and she turned away so Holly wouldn't notice and tease her about it . . . or worse, ask questions that Kate wasn't ready to answer. From behind the old barn, a giant backhoe rumbled into view. The guy driving it waved.

"Don't come any closer," he yelled.

Holly yelled back. "We're not." She prodded Kate with her boot and said, "Are we?"

"No way," Kate replied.

For a horse, Tapestry was quite brave. She could deal with almost anything except coops and chickens, which totally freaked her out. But Kate wasn't too sure about yellow backhoes that looked like dinosaurs with rocks and mud spilling from their jaws. Tapestry snorted. So did Magician.

"Copycat," Holly said.

Kate rolled her eyes. Their two horses were totally in sync. What one did, the other did as well. In the back paddock, they'd stand nose to tail, flicking flies off each other for hours on end. In the barn, they nibbled one another's manes over their stall partition. And Magician wouldn't even load onto the trailer unless Tapestry was already onboard. They were each other's best friend.

Just like Kate and Holly.

* * *

Holly took the lead as they rode home. Dappled sunlight filtered through a canopy of trees; pine needles and ferns carpeted the trail. Two squirrels darted across it. Magician skittered sideways, then shied at a moss-covered rock he'd seen a million times before. It happened so fast that Holly almost lost her balance. Her mind was elsewhere, puzzled about that farm they'd just seen.

"Easy boy," she said.

When they reached the hunt course, Holly aimed her black gelding at the first fence and he popped over it as if it were no bigger than a shoe box. Kate rode beside her. Around the field they went, clearing brush jumps, logs, ditches, and rustic rails.

"That was fun," Holly said, patting Magician's sweaty neck. "But you cheated."

"How?"

"You did all the lower jumps."

"That's because you hogged the higher ones," Kate said. "Let's do it again, and this time—"

"No, let's do the cross-country course."

It was a whole lot more challenging than the hunt course, and they hadn't ridden it since before going to England back in June. Plus it would take her mind off Sam Callahan's fancy new show barn. Well, not exactly fancy, but Holly was sure it would be when the famous trainer got through fixing it up. According to his Facebook page, he'd already transformed two barns down in North Carolina and another in Massachusetts. His riders won all the top prizes.

"Good idea," Kate said, grinning. "And I'll beat you."

"No racing," Holly warned.

Last summer Kate had almost gotten herself kicked out of Timber Ridge when Angela Dean, who'd bullied and taunted Kate ever since she'd arrived, had challenged her to a race over the cross-country jumps. Angela had won, but only because she'd veered off course and jumped a barbed-wire fence. Kate had pulled up just in time.

So, of course, Angela had boasted about her win all over the barn, and Mom had been furious with both of them. Bad enough they'd broken the rules, but Kate had done it riding Buccaneer. Back then, he'd belonged to the movie director Giles Ballantine, who'd shot part of *Moonlight* at Timber Ridge.

Kate said, "Only kidding."

"You go first."

Holly held Magician firmly in check as Tapestry leaped forward. Legs neatly tucked, Kate's golden mare jumped the rustic panel. Watching Tapestry now, it was hard to remember what a mess she'd been when Kate had rescued her from the kill truck a year ago.

The skeptics said you couldn't take a "dollar horse" and turn it into a winner, but that was exactly what Kate had done. But she'd had good material to work with. Hidden beneath the dull coat and overgrown hooves was a chestnut Morgan with a flaxen mane and tail. Other skeptics said that Morgans couldn't jump or do dressage, but Kate had proved them wrong as well.

Magician chomped at the bit, eager to catch up with his best buddy.

"Okay, let's rock it," Holly said.

In three strides, they cleared the panel with room to spare. Tightening her grip, Holly leaned into Magician's flying mane and headed for the next fence—two railroad ties above a ditch. Yesterday's showers had left puddles on the trail. Her horse galloped through them, not caring a whit about getting splashed.

Magician loved water.

As she was soaring over the jump, Holly caught sight of Kate about to plunge into the stream. Magician neighed. Tapestry neighed back, and Holly laughed. These two horses were so predictable.

"Come on in," Kate yelled.

Magician needed no urging. He slithered down the muddy bank and into the stream, and almost immediately Holly could feel his legs buckle. Down went Magician's front end. His hindquarters collapsed, and before Holly knew it, she was leaping free of her horse.

And just in time, too.

She watched helplessly as Magician wriggled happily

in the water, soaking his saddle and bridle. She'd have a fun time getting *them* clean and dry and her riding boots, too.

Kate grinned. "He got you again, huh?"

"And how," Holly said, grinning back.

If anyone knew what this felt like, Kate did. She'd ridden Magician over the cross-country course in her screen test for the stunt-double role in *Moonlight*. The director had loved Magician's unscripted dip in the stream so much that he'd included it in the final film.

Later, when Kate rode the scene again, she'd worn a gauzy white dress with long scarves that floated from her shoulders, just like a fairy princess. Holly gave herself a little pinch. She was too old to believe in fairytales, but sometimes it was fun to fantasize about magic and sparkles and . . .

In a flash, Magician brought her back to earth. Scrambling to his feet, he shook himself so violently that Holly got even wetter than she already was. She kissed Magician's velvety black nose and pretended to be a princess anyway—a very wet princess.

* * *

The last thing Twiggy felt like was a princess. Not a barn princess—that was Angela Dean's job—but "Princess Isabel of Lunaberg."

A totally useless title.

She'd been stuck with it since birth, never mind that her family's tiny European country had vanished during the Napoleonic Wars over two hundred years ago. Her father cared about all this historical stuff; Twiggy didn't. She only cared about horses . . . and her new best friends.

She'd never had any best friends before.

All the girls at her stuffy old boarding school in England had either scorned her for being different or treated her with kid gloves—like royalty—which she was.

But she didn't want to be.

Life was much better in Vermont, where she mucked stalls, cleaned tack, and worked her buns off to make the Timber Ridge riding team. And so far, nobody had cared—well, except for Angela and her snooty mother—if she were a princess or a pineapple.

After scooping up the last pile of manure from Chantilly's empty stall, Twiggy dragged her muck bucket into the aisle. She wiped a strand of blond hair off her sweaty face and propped her pitchfork against the wall, where it promptly fell over.

It was just over a week since she'd arrived at Timber Ridge, but already it felt more like a year. A lot had happened—an awful lot—and she'd managed to hide most of it from her father, at home in London.

None of it had been her fault. Just stuff that she'd had no control over—like her new bodyguard, Meredith Tudor, getting whacked in the head by a runaway horse.

Okay, so Meredith had survived and was recuperating just fine, and the horse had belonged to Luke Callahan, the stunningly swoon-worthy show jumper. But that hadn't counted with her father.

He'd forbidden Twiggy to ride the trails without her bodyguard, which meant she hadn't been able to go out with Holly and Kate earlier. He'd even threatened to drag Twiggy home—right back to England and the claustro-phobic life that she hated. They were still negotiating on this, but—

"Hi," said a voice. "Who are you?"

Twiggy whipped around so fast, she tripped on her pitchfork and fell over. "I'm a klutz," she said, looking up at a girl she'd never seen before.

"Hello, Klutz. I'm a robin."

Robin?

Oh, yes, the girl who'd been gone all summer, out west some place. She owned the dappled gray mare whose stall Twiggy had just cleaned.

Still smiling, Robin held out her hand and hauled Twiggy to her feet. "You've got manure on your backside. And where's everyone else? There's a riding team lesson in ten minutes. If we hustle, we can make it." She gave Twiggy a puzzled look, almost as if she knew who Twiggy was but wanted to make sure. "What's your real name?"

2

TWIGGY WAITED for the inevitable questions, the wide-eyed expression when the penny finally dropped, and the dreaded, "Oh, my gosh, you're a *real* princess!"

When she'd first arrived at Timber Ridge, one of the younger kids had actually curtsied. Another had asked if Twiggy knew Kate Middleton and Prince William. She did, but she never talked about it because that would be tacky—even worse than wearing her tiara at school on prize-giving day, but that was only because Mum had insisted.

The. Absolute. Pits.

"I'm Isabel DuBois," Twiggy said, wiping both hands on her jeans and offering the cleanest one to Robin. Her father always insisted she shake hands with people, no matter what. "But everyone calls me Twiggy."

"Let me guess," Robin said. She frowned and put a finger to her lips.

Twiggy waited. Not many people made the connection, unless they spoke French. Her father's nickname was *Root*, but his real name was Prince Ferdinand, like the bull—except Dad was tall and thin with bushy eyebrows, more like a fierce giraffe than a friendly bull.

"DuBois," Robin said. "*Of the wood?*"

Delightedly, Twiggy nodded. She liked this girl whose name could be either a boy's or a girl's and who didn't know who Twiggy was—well, unless Robin was faking it. But that didn't seem likely, because why would she? Besides, she'd find out soon enough.

"Chantilly's outside," Twiggy said. "But I left her halter on."

"Thanks," Robin said. "She can be hard to catch."

"I know," Twiggy said. "She led me a merry dance the other day."

Still talking, they headed for the paddock where Chantilly was grazing with Marmalade and the ponies. Robin produced cookies, and immediately Plug muscled his way in, demanding more than his fair share. Twiggy patted the pony's fuzzy brown nose.

If only Diamond were here.

He was bright bay with a tiny star on his forehead, so faint you could barely see it, and Twiggy loved him to death. If he were at Timber Ridge, life would be perfect.

But Diamond was back in England, which was where Twiggy would be soon if she couldn't convince her father to let her stay. If only he'd send Diamond over as well.

No, that was impossible. Dad would never ship him over, never mind he could afford to hire grooms and charter an entire jet to do it. On second thought, he could use his own jet. It was certainly big enough. Her cell phone rang.

Dad?

Was he calling to say it was okay for her to stay at Timber Ridge, or was he demanding that she come home, like right away? Firmly, Twiggy pushed Plug to one side and dug the phone from her pocket. Grain, bits of hay, and a wizened carrot erupted. Quick as a wink, Plug vacuumed them up.

Twiggy checked caller ID, then crossed her fingers.

* * *

Kate's heart gave a little twist of pleasure the way it always did when the Timber Ridge barn came into view. Ever since she'd arrived a year ago, it had felt like home, unlike her old barn in Connecticut where she'd learned to ride.

Best not to think about that.

The memories of Black Magic were still too raw, and Mrs. Mueller's accusations still lurked in the far corners of Kate's brain.

You killed my horse.

But she hadn't. Another girl had neglected to latch Magic's stall door that terrible night. He'd gotten out and let himself into the feed room where he'd gorged on grain, colicked, and died before anyone found him.

A bead of sweat trickled down Kate's face; her head itched. She pulled off her helmet and shook out her shoulder length brown hair. It would be so much cooler to ride without a helmet like she had in her *Moonlight* scene, but Liz would ground her if she did.

Kate shoved her helmet back on, then looked at their familiar barn again. It reminded her of the one they'd just seen—faded red clapboards and a lopsided weathervane on the roof—but unlike that mysterious old barn in the woods, Timber Ridge glowed with life.

Ponies grazed in the paddock, flowers tumbled from window boxes, and four riders circled Liz Chapman in the outdoor ring. Holly's mom—now Kate's stepmother—ran the barn, and she was the best riding instructor Kate had ever had. Then again, she'd only had two, but she'd taken lots of clinics and had spent a month in England, training with former Olympic riders.

Shading her eyes, Kate picked out Angela Dean on her bay warmblood, Ragtime, trotting behind her best friend, Kristina James, whose palomino, Cody, was tossing his head. Then came Twiggy on Jennifer West's chestnut gelding, Rebel. But who was riding Chantilly?

"Is that Robin?" Holly said.

Kate looked again. "Yeah, I think so."

This meant the Timber Ridge riding team was almost complete. Only Jennifer was missing. She was still in England at Beaumont Park, her grandmother's famous equestrian center where Kate and Holly had—

"Nice of you to stop by," Liz yelled.

Arms folded, she tapped a foot as they rode toward the ring, and Kate had a horrible feeling they'd messed up. For the past week, Liz had been drilling them hard every day, but Kate was sure that she'd checked the lesson schedule and that nothing was listed for this afternoon, which had left her and Holly free to ride the trails.

"Uh, oh," Holly muttered.

"Guess we're in for it, now," Kate said. Even though she and Holly were family, Liz cut them no slack. If anything, she was tougher on them than she was on the others. As they drew closer, Kate could see that Liz's blue eyes, so much like Holly's, were narrowed and angry looking.

Liz told them to put their horses away and wait in her office. There'd be a meeting as soon as she was finished with the team riding lesson. And could they please explain why they had missed it?

"But, Mom," Holly wailed. "We didn't know. It wasn't on the board."

"Wrong," Liz said. "Check it again."

But when they did, Holly said, "That's not Mom's writing."

Leaning across Liz's untidy desk, Kate peered at the white board. Holly was right. Those loops and flourishes looked nothing like Liz's scribble. Half the time you couldn't read her writing, but this was actually legible.

Almost too legible.

"Angela," Holly said. "I bet she erased Mom's entry this morning, then put it back after you and I left the barn."

Miserably, Kate nodded. Angela had done this before and gotten Kate into a boatload of trouble. Was she up to her old tricks again? And if so, why?

Just then, Twiggy bounced into the office, still holding Rebel's saddle. She dumped it onto Liz's wobbly swivel chair. "Hey, guys. You'll never guess, but—"

"What?" Holly said.

"Dad's gonna let me stay."

"Whoot!" Holly shrieked.

Her wet boots left muddy tracks on the floor as she danced Twiggy around Liz's cramped office, and Kate wondered where the princess would live. She'd been staying at Angela's house but not loving it.

And what about Meredith Tudor?

Mrs. Dean hadn't exactly given Twiggy's African American bodyguard a warm welcome, never mind that she'd once been a hugely successful dressage rider.

* * *

"Okay, girls," Liz said, leaning against her desk. "Listen up." She shifted sideways, and a pile of papers slid onto the dusty floor. Kate gathered them up—old invoices, delivery notices, and a spreadsheet dated six months ago. She stacked them neatly on a free corner of Liz's messy desk.

Angela lounged in the doorway, one expensively shod foot propped against the frame as if she were ready to take off at any minute. With an elaborate sigh, she tossed back a wave of shiny black hair.

"Will this take all day?"

Beside her, Kristina smirked. She wasn't brave enough to challenge Liz the way Angela did, but her sulky attitude spoke volumes.

"That depends," Liz said.

"On what?"

"On whether or not you pay attention."

"Yeah, what*ever*," Angela drawled. Her icy blue eyes turned venomous as Holly took a step forward. But Twiggy got there first.

"That's rude," she said, wagging her finger at Angela like an old-fashioned schoolteacher. "Say you're sorry."

Kate suppressed a giggle.

This wouldn't go down well with Angela or her bossy mother. Maybe they'd suspend Twiggy's Internet privileges, toss her into the street, or—

"Sor-*reee*," Angela said.

Ignoring her, Liz said, "We've got another big event coming up."

"The Labor Day show?" Kate asked.

It supported Mrs. Dean's favorite charity, and last year's show was the first one that Kate had competed in with Tapestry. They'd had a surprise win over Angela in junior jumping, and Holly had won blue when she'd gone head-to-head in Gambler's Choice with her boyfriend, Adam, who rode for Larchwood.

"No," Liz replied. "The Vermont Summer Classic."

A bazillion thoughts tumbled through Kate's head. This event was invitation only. Your team had to be really good to qualify. Maybe another team had dropped out at the last minute, and the organizers were scrambling to make up the numbers. But that didn't make any sense. They had their pick of teams. No, it had to be something else.

"When is it?" Robin said.

Liz gave a little sigh, as if she wasn't happy about this unscheduled show landing in her lap. "The weekend after next."

Quickly, Kate did the math. They had nine days to get ready—not nearly enough time. The Vermont show was even bigger than last year's Hampshire Classic, where—despite Angela's best attempts at sabotage—Kate had helped Timber Ridge to win first place. But this summer,

Kate and Holly had been in England, and the riding team had flubbed up. Mrs. Dean had even yelled at Angela. So, what on earth was Liz thinking?

It had to be Mrs. Dean.

Bribery was her middle name. Somehow, she'd pulled favors and wangled a spot at this super prestigious show, forcing Liz to get the team ready sooner than expected. They'd been gearing up, slowly and carefully for the Labor Day Show, and having this one shoehorned into their routine would mess up Liz's well-organized training schedule. Plus, with Jennifer West still in England, they were one rider short.

But Angela's mother didn't care.

To her, it was all about the trophies, medals, and blue ribbons the riding team won. She displayed them in a glass case at the Timber Ridge clubhouse and told anyone who'd listen that her daughter was the team's superstar, that without Angela's brilliant riding there would be no trophies, no ribbons.

A lump got stuck in Kate's throat.

Her mother, who'd died six years ago when Kate was nine, always said, "It's not about winning blue ribbons. It's about doing your best and feeling good about yourself."

"You okay?" Holly whispered.

"Yeah." Kate wiped her eyes. Thinking about Mom always made her cry. She shot a look at Angela, but she hadn't noticed. She was too busy showing her latest manicure to Kristina.

Twiggy had backed off and was now sitting on a sawhorse beside Robin. With Robin home, Liz had more riders to choose from, which was great. Holly's Aunt Bea had picked the last Timber Ridge team, but she was on a book tour promoting her latest mystery and wouldn't be back until two days before the show. So, who would pick it this time?

As if reading Kate's mind, Liz said, "Meredith Tudor has kindly offered to choose the team. There will be three of you, with one reserve rider."

"What's that?" Angela said.

Liz checked her notes. "The reserve will take over if another horse or rider is injured and unable to complete the event."

"Even in the middle of it?"

"Yes," Liz said. "And selection takes place on Monday."

"What sort of competition is it?" Twiggy said.

Technically, she wasn't part of the riding team because she wasn't a resident of Timber Ridge, but Mrs. Dean— who made up the rules as she went along—had made it quite clear that her *royal* guest was welcome to join, unlike Kate who'd been blocked by Mrs. Dean at every turn.

But not any more.

Thanks to Dad marrying Liz, Kate was now an official resident—unless Mrs. Dean found a way to mess that up as well.

Liz pulled a stack of papers from her printer and handed them out. "This will explain the event. It's similar to the Festival of Horses—dressage, cross country, jumping, and stable management. There won't be a written test."

"Phew," Kristina said, wiping her brow.

Liz looked at her, then at all the girls, letting her gaze rest for a few seconds longer on Angela. "But there will be horsemanship."

"What's that?" Kristina said.

Angela snorted. "Something dumb, I bet."

"It's in the rules," Liz said. "I suggest you read them carefully, and there's more information on the web site." She stood up. "Now, we've got a lot of work to do in order to be ready, and I want everyone's full cooperation—whether or not you make the final team."

"Are we done yet?" Angela said.

From the self-satisfied look on her face, it was clear that Angela already knew she'd be chosen for the team. Her mother would make sure of that, no matter who was doing the choosing.

3

As she walked toward Tapestry's stall, Kate couldn't stop thinking about Angela and her nonchalant reaction to the Vermont Classic. It was like she already knew about it.

Well, hello?

Of course, she did. And this was why she'd erased Liz's note about the team's riding lesson, just to rattle Kate. It was childish and stupid. But Angela had pulled the same stunt last year. With a bit of creative rescheduling on the white board, Angela had caused Kate to blow off two beginner lessons that Liz had been counting on her to teach.

Not a happy moment.

Kate gave the horse show papers a cursory glance and stuffed them into her pocket. They could wait until later. Then she opened Tapestry's door and found Marcia Dean hard at work. Dust flew in all directions as Marcia expertly wielded her rubber curry comb over Tapestry's golden coat.

"Hi," Marcia said.

At almost twelve, Angela's former stepsister was petite with a freckled, elfin face and frizzy red curls that bounced like springs as she worked. For a moment, Kate just stood there, soaking it up. Here was another girl who loved Tapestry as much as she did, and it made her feel warm and fuzzy inside. Marcia was nothing like Angela, who never picked up a brush if she could get someone else to do it for her.

Until last year, that "someone" had always been Marcia. Like a real-life Cinderella, she'd quietly groomed Angela's horses, cleaned their tack, and mucked stalls. But nobody had paid attention, especially Mrs. Dean, who expected Marcia to do it all without any praise or hint of reward, like a pony of her own.

Marcia had finally snapped. Without telling anyone, she'd taken off with Angela's horse to prove she could ride as well as her stepsister and had gotten herself dumped on the hunt course in a freak Halloween blizzard.

Kate and Holly had rescued her.

And now Marcia's father, who had tons of money and was super grateful to Kate and Holly for saving his daughter, wanted to buy Tapestry for Marcia—or lease her.

They'd danced around this issue for months, but Kate

couldn't bring herself to make a decision. Everyone said it was a great opportunity. With a lease, Tapestry would stay at the barn, Kate would get to ride her whenever she wanted, and Mr. Dean would pick up the tab. It also meant that Kate could afford to lease another horse for herself. Well, maybe, if the terms were right and she was lucky enough to find the right horse.

But selling Tapestry?

No way.

Never mind that Mr. Dean had offered her a small fortune and Liz had already pointed out that if Kate wanted to move forward in her quest to become a better rider, she needed a better horse. It was a hard pill to swallow because Tapestry was everything Kate had ever dreamed of in a horse—and more. She would never sell her.

Marcia turned and grinned, revealing a mouth full of brand-new hardware and a rainbow of elastics.

"How's it going?" Kate said.

She'd gotten rid of her own braces the year before she moved to Timber Ridge. Last week, when she was having her wisdom tooth pulled, the dentist had complimented her bite and said her teeth were awesome. Well, except for the one she was about to lose.

"Okay," Marcia said, grinning even wider. "I'm gonna use the elastics to braid Tapestry's mane when I'm done with them." She rubbed the mare's withers. "Did you get in trouble?"

"For missing the lesson?"

"Yeah." Marcia dropped her curry comb into Kate's grooming box and snagged a hoof pick. She leaned against Tapestry, who obligingly lifted her left foreleg. "I bet Liz yelled at you."

"Nope," Kate said. "Not this time."

Instead, Liz had yelled at Angela. Well, not exactly yelled, but after the meeting she'd told Angela to stay behind. Even before the door to her office had closed, Kate heard Liz telling Angela, quite sternly, to keep her hands off the white board.

"Good," Holly had said before leading Magician out to the back paddock. "It's about time Mom stood up for herself."

That was the trouble.

If Liz confronted Angela, Mrs. Dean got on her high horse and threatened to fire Liz. But if Liz allowed Angela to get away with cheating, it set a rotten example to everyone else and made Liz look like a wimp.

A no-win situation.

"Want me to turn Tapestry out?" Marcia said, unclipping Tapestry's lead rope from the wall.

"Yeah, sure," Kate replied. "And, thanks."

After Marcia and Tapestry trundled off, Kate parked herself on a tack trunk. Something rustled.

Oh, yeah. The paperwork.

She'd better read it and find out what they were letting

themselves in for. On the second page was a list of all the teams who'd been chosen to compete, including Larchwood, Fox Meadow, and Spruce Hill Farm.

No surprise there.

Kate had competed against them before. They were good, really good, especially Larchwood where Adam rode. Holly was always trying to get him to switch teams and ride for Timber Ridge instead. He always refused. It was more fun, he insisted, to ride *against* Holly than to ride *with* her.

Kate scanned the list again. It was in alphabetic order, and the last entry caught her eye.

Weathervane Farm?

No, surely not. Sam Callahan's new barn was a wreck. It would take months and months to get it fixed up and ready for horses. This was probably another farm with the same name, which wasn't unusual. There was even another Timber Ridge over in Maine, but it was a Western barn. They didn't compete in the same shows.

Ten minutes later, as she walked back to the house with Holly, Kate fished out her list and pointed at the last entry. "Did you see this?"

"Pfftt," Holly said, grinning. She turned and waved toward the rusty weathervane atop their own barn. "Every farm in New England has one of those. It's not exactly an original name, is it?"

Kate shrugged. "I guess."

"Cheer up," Holly said, poking Kate's arm. "If it really is the same farm, you'll get to see Luke again."

Something else to worry about.

Luke Callahan.

She really liked him, but just because he'd said nice things about her horse didn't mean he thought Kate was cute or interesting.

Cute?

That label belonged to Holly. She had sparkling blue eyes, streaky blond hair, and a bubbly personality that everyone loved. Oh, and she was funny and smart, too. Kate gave a little sigh. She would have to settle for *interesting*, which was fine with her.

* * *

For the tenth time in as many minutes, Twiggy looked at the ornate clock on Mrs. Dean's sideboard. Dinner had already lasted for what felt like hours, and they hadn't even gotten to dessert yet because Angela's mother kept asking silly questions.

"What's the palace like?" she said.

"Which one?" Twiggy replied, just to be annoying. She knew exactly which one Mrs. Dean meant, even though there were dozens of palaces in England.

"Bucking-*ham* Palace," said Mrs. Dean, mispronouncing it like all Americans did. "Where the queen lives."

"It's gray on the outside, red and gold on the inside,

and it's *h-u-u-u-g-e*," Twiggy said. "You need a map to get around."

Angela's eyes widened. "Have you been there?"

"Yup."

This produced another flood of questions, but all Twiggy wanted was to get through dinner so she could escape upstairs and play Scrabble with Meredith. Last night, she'd almost beaten her.

"Tell us about it," said Mrs. Dean.

Twiggy sighed. "The queen gave my father a medal, and I watched."

"Oh, how exciting," said Mrs. Dean. "What was the medal for?"

"He didn't tell us," Twiggy replied, spearing a piece of hated broccoli and almost choking on it. "Something secret, I guess."

Dad worked for the government but never talked about his job. Dressed in a dark suit and carrying a black umbrella, Prince Ferdinand left the house at eight thirty every morning, climbed into a black limousine, and joined the rest of London heading off to work. It was all rather hush-hush. Not even Mum knew what he did.

"He's a spy?" Angela squealed.

Twiggy shrugged. If her father was a spy, he wasn't a very good one, given that he knew nothing about Twiggy running away from boarding school. She'd make a much better spy than he did. The queen should've given *her* a medal, not Dad.

"Like James Bond," said Mrs. Dean. "And the CIA."

"The CIA is American, not British," Angela retorted. She shot a look at Twiggy that said, *Parents can be so stupid.*

But Mrs. Dean didn't look the least bit embarrassed over her gaffe. "Same thing," she said airily.

Much to Twiggy's relief, dessert arrived. She inhaled a bowl of chocolate mousse, faked a theatrical yawn, and claimed she was ready for bed. "That was a yummy meal, but I really am tired."

"Me, too," said Angela.

Twiggy faked another yawn, then fled upstairs to her bodyguard's room, hoping that Angela wouldn't follow or barge in without knocking the way she had the other night.

Meredith was sitting by the window with a meal tray on her lap when Twiggy arrived, breathless. She locked the door and leaned against it.

"How was dinner?" Meredith said.

"Ghastly," Twiggy replied. "I had to eat broccoli. What are you having?"

"Eggplant."

"What's that?"

"You Brits call it 'aubergine,'" Meredith said. She held out a forkful. "Want some?"

"No, thanks," Twiggy said, shuddering. She liked this veggie even less than she liked broccoli.

"Okay." Meredith smiled, showing dazzlingly white

teeth that all Americans seemed to have. Twiggy vowed to do a better job of brushing hers. Maybe she'd even get braces like Marcia Dean, except they didn't look very comfortable.

"How's your head?" Twiggy flung herself onto Meredith's bed, strewn with dressage books about Charlotte Dujardin and her horse, Valegro. He was so famous, he even had his own Facebook page.

"Much better," Meredith said. "I'll be choosing the riding team on Monday."

"Yeah, Liz told us," Twiggy said. "But I'm not good enough to make it, so—"

"Don't worry. I won't play favorites." Meredith's smile dimmed. "There's something I have to tell you."

"You can ride with me again?"

"Yes, but not for much longer," Meredith said. She set aside her tray and stood up. "I've been offered another job."

"But you've already got one," Twiggy said, alarmed. Meredith was the best bodyguard she'd ever had—far more fun than dumb old Stefan. All he ever did was watch noisy cop shows on TV and cruise around in Dad's gigantic black limo. Half the time, he didn't even bother to go with her when she went shopping or visited friends, and he hardly ever came to the stables. But Twiggy didn't rat on him to Dad because she preferred it that way.

There was a pause, then Meredith said, "I know, and

I've loved being with you, but this is a great opportunity."

Tears welled up. Wiping them away, Twiggy braced herself. She was no stranger to bad news. "Tell me," she whispered.

"Sam Callahan is opening a new barn, and he wants me to run it." With a sigh, Meredith turned toward the window, as if she couldn't bear to see Twiggy's mournful face. "And I'll get to compete again."

"When are you leaving?"

"As soon as your new bodyguard gets here."

4

FOR A MOMENT, Holly stared at her phone. Twiggy hadn't been too coherent—lots of sniffling and crying—but Holly had finally gotten the message before Twiggy hung up.

She glanced at Kate, sprawled across her bed, reading the latest *Dressage Today*. "You're not gonna like this."

"What?" Kate didn't look up.

"It's about that old farm."

"Sam Callahan's place?"

"Yes," Holly said. "Meredith's going to work for him, like next week, and—"

Kate sat up so fast that two pages ripped from her magazine. "You're kidding, right?"

"No, I'm dead serious," Holly said, gathering up two stuffed ponies and hugging them. She twisted the pinto's tail around her fingers. "But I figured it would happen."

"How?" Kate said. "When?"

"At the hospital, when Mr. Callahan said he had the perfect dressage horse for Meredith to ride," Holly said, then remembered that Kate hadn't been there because of her tooth. It was just Holly and Twiggy and Sam Callahan at the ER, waiting for news about Meredith. The riding helmet she'd been wearing had probably saved her from serious brain damage. That's what the docs said, anyway.

"You never told me." Kate sounded huffy.

Holly shrugged. "Sorry, I forgot."

It was such a minor detail in all the confusion of that scary day. Without telling Twiggy's bodyguard the reason why, Holly had convinced her to drive both girls to a horse show so that Holly could confront Sam Callahan about why Meredith had been banned from competition. He would be sure to know the answer, and Holly was even more sure that his answer would clear Meredith's name.

But before she had a chance to ask, two things happened at once: Twiggy slipped and landed in the mud, and Luke's horse got loose. In a flash, Meredith had thrown herself on top of Twiggy and gotten whacked on the head by Santiago's hoof as he'd thundered past.

There was a lengthy pause, then Kate said, "I'm glad Meredith's got a job with Sam Callahan, but they won't be ready in time for the show."

"Twiggy said they will." Holly hugged her ponies even harder. Why was Kate so tweaked about Weathervane Farm? Was she scared of getting beaten or scared of her feelings for Luke? That was probably it. Kate was fabulous with horses but hopeless when it came to guys.

"Okay, but how?" Kate said.

"Sam Callahan's renting barn space at Larchwood till his own farm is ready, so that's where Meredith will be working."

Kate retrieved her magazine from the floor. Several seconds went by as she tried to stick the torn pages back in again. "Lucky Adam."

Was Kate being sarcastic? Holly couldn't tell. There were times when Kate kept her feelings buttoned up so tight that you almost needed a crowbar to pry them loose.

"You know what this means, don't you?" said Holly.

Her sister shrugged.

"We've got to work even harder if we're gonna beat those guys," Holly said, then decided not to mention that Kate's magazine was now upside down.

* * *

Being a sister was a whole harder than Kate had imagined. It had been much easier when she and Holly were best friends and living in different houses, rather than sharing a tiny bedroom that stayed cluttered no matter how many times Kate tidied it up. If Dad and Liz were able to buy the house from Mrs. Dean, they would add another bedroom.

Kate couldn't wait.

With an exasperated sigh, she whisked Holly's torn breeches off her rocking horse, stuffed the ponies back in their hammock, and filled a laundry basket with socks, underwear, jeans, and t-shirts that her sister had dumped carelessly on the floor last night. Kate hauled everything into the basement and left it there because Dad hadn't finished fixing the pipes.

Tools and parts littered the workbench; a trail of greasy fingerprints crawled across the washing machine. Tonight she'd suggest that Dad call a plumber.

It had always been this way.

Professor McGregor pretty much lived on another planet, lost in the esoteric world of rare moths and butterflies, far away from broken appliances and flat tires. Half the time, he wasn't even home. So Mom had taken care of household problems, but after she died, they'd fallen on Kate's nine-year-old shoulders. She'd looked after Dad, cooking and cleaning as best she could and reminding him to pay the car insurance and gas bill.

Her stomach growled. Kate made a quick pass through the kitchen and grabbed a blueberry muffin. It was later than she'd thought, almost nine thirty. A half-empty mug of cold coffee sat on the counter, proof that Liz had already left. She was probably at the barn with Holly.

Kate rode her bike—quicker than walking. But when she pedaled up to the barn a few minutes later, Liz and Holly weren't there—just Marcia and her best friend Laura Gardner, grooming Laura's fcisty rcd pony, Soupçon, on the crossties.

"Liz went to the feed store," Marcia said, brushing vigorously. The pony curled his lip.

Laura chimed in. "And Holly's with the *princess*."

Both girls giggled. Like all the younger kids, they were beyond thrilled to have a real-life princess in the barn. If it were up to them, Twiggy would wear frothy ball gowns, twinkly shoes, and a tiara instead of grubby t-shirts and muck boots.

"Where are they?" Kate said.

More giggles. "Out riding."

A ginger barn cat streaked down the aisle, tail fluffed up like a bottle brush. Kate stepped out of its way and looked around. Magician's stall was empty. No wonder Tapestry was banging on her door. She hated being left behind.

So did Kate.

Taking a deep breath, she inhaled the heady aroma of horses and reminded herself for the millionth time that it was okay for Holly to do stuff on her own. They weren't joined at the hip. So why did Kate feel excluded?

She kicked at a clump of manure and slouched toward the tack room. Maybe she'd hack out and find them. They couldn't have gone far. The doc had told Meredith to take it easy for a few more days, which meant she'd be riding Marmalade, who never went faster than a slow trot.

But when she looked, Marmalade was grazing in the back paddock with Daisy, and two other horses besides Magician had gone missing—Rebel and Ragtime.

Ragtime?

Nobody, except Angela, was allowed to ride him. Kate frowned. Twiggy had been ordered *not* to ride the trails without her bodyguard. This meant she'd either disobeyed her father—and Angela had gone with her and Holly—or Meredith had borrowed Ragtime without permission.

Whatever.

It wasn't her problem. Prince Ferdinand wasn't likely to swoop down like an angry eagle, blame Kate, and fly her back to England. Although, on second thought, it would be kind of neat if he did. She'd loved it over there and she missed Buccaneer like mad. It was nothing short of a miracle that he'd wound up at Beaumont Park.

Without thinking, Kate checked her pockets for Life Savers—Buccaneer's favorite treat—but all she found were crumpled tissues and a tube of orange lip balm. Tapestry thought it was a carrot.

Kate brushed her mare, not putting much effort into it, then saddled her up and took off. Which direction? Toward the hunt course or around the other side of the mountain where she'd first seen Tapestry, locked up in the crazy old hermit's backyard?

Or how about Weathervane Farm?

Even if Kate didn't find the others, she wanted to take another look at Sam Callahan's new show barn, even if it was a tumbledown mess.

* * *

Twiggy still couldn't get over it. Angela offering Ragtime to Meredith? At first, she hadn't believed her, but Angela kept insisting. So had Mrs. Dean. Now that Meredith's name had been cleared and she was going to ride for the famous Sam Callahan, it was a whole different story. Mrs. Dean would probably beg her to coach Angela.

The phony.

Angela's mother had been so horrible to Meredith that Twiggy had wanted to smack her. She would have, too, if Holly hadn't told her to keep cool. There were better ways of defeating Mrs. Dean.

"Like what?" Twiggy had said.

"Dunno, but we'll figure something out."

The trail opened up into a large, sloping meadow scattered with rustic fences that Holly said was the Timber Ridge hunt course. Twiggy had hunted in England, but only because they weren't allowed to chase foxes and deer anymore. No way did she want to watch hounds killing Bambi or a poor little fox, never mind if they stole people's chickens.

Anxious to follow Magician, Rebel danced about and

pulled at his bit. Twiggy let him go but aimed for the lower part of each fence. Over the crossrails, the brush jump, the logs and ditches they went. Twiggy's confidence rose. Maybe she'd try the bigger ones, but Meredith shook her head.

"Not on a horse you don't know."

"Spoilsport," Twiggy muttered, but Meredith was right. It would be just her luck to try something she wasn't ready for, knock herself senseless, and have Dad swooping over here to fetch her back home.

"Hey, look over there," Holly yelled, bringing Magician to a halt. She pointed toward the trail they'd just been on.

Twiggy scrunched up her eyes. "What?"

"A fox."

Something brownish-gray with perky ears and a long, bushy tail looked at them for a moment, then slunk out of sight, swallowed up by trees and undergrowth.

"Kind of big for a fox," Meredith said.

"He was huge," Holly agreed. "More like a coyote."

"Wow." Twiggy stood up in her stirrups, hoping for another glimpse. This was super exciting. She'd never seen a coyote before. She hadn't even known how to pronounce it properly. Some American words were so peculiar.

"Odd, though," Meredith said. "You don't normally see coyotes in the middle of the day, unless—"

"What?" Twiggy said.

"They're rabid."

Ah yes, rabies. Something else America had that England didn't. As they rode back to the barn, Twiggy kept a lookout in case that coyote reappeared. It was all so different here, and excitingly strange. The bridle trails she'd ridden in England had well-groomed footing, big old shade trees, and masses of bluebells in the Spring. It was like riding in a park.

This was the wild, wild wood.

An owl hooted; stones and last year's leaves crunched underfoot. Vines, thick as climbing ropes in a gym, spiraled down and narrowly missed Twiggy's face. She fended them off, then Rebel shied at a moss-covered rock that looked like a giant frog. Overhead, the canopy of pines was so dense that only a few shafts of dazzling sunlight hit the ground. It was like riding through an enchanted tunnel.

But a coyote?

This was a story to tell the snotty girls at school. Twiggy pulled a sour face. Her old life was far, far away— and right now she wanted it to stay there.

5

IT FELT KIND OF ODD to be alone on the trail without Holly. But Kate didn't feel alone. Eyes were watching her, tracking her progress toward Sam Callahan's farm. Hundreds of eyes.

Well, duh-uh.

Of course there were hundreds of eyes. Probably thousands. She was in the woods surrounded by insects and birds and small animals, most of which she couldn't see and probably couldn't even identify. But Kate couldn't shake off the feeling that one pair of eyes was more vigilant than the others, more watchful—

More dangerous?

Feeling like an idiot, Kate pulled herself together. She was getting beyond silly. There was nothing on the Timber Ridge trails that could hurt her, except for an out-of-control mountain biker or Tapestry having a meltdown over a plastic bag and dumping her on a rock.

She leaned forward. "Are you okay?"

If she wasn't, Kate would find out soon enough. And if there *was* something out there, Tapestry would go on full alert. She'd dig in her toes, then whip around and race back the way they'd just come. Horses were smart like that. They didn't stand up to danger; they ran away from it.

Kate whistled, she hummed a little.

She tried a few words of whatever song it was that Holly had been playing on her iPod speakers last night. Okay, she was off key, but who cared? Nobody could hear her.

Except Tapestry. Her ears swiveled like antennae.

"Sorry," Kate said, patting her.

Crash!

Tapestry snorted and whirled around so fast that Kate almost fell off. "Easy, girl. Easy," she said, hauling herself back into the saddle. Okay so what was it? What was big enough to make a noise like that?

A bear?

Holly said they were all over the mountain. Black bears. The nice kind—unless it was a mother and her cubs, and then all bets were off. Tapestry quivered; she darted sideways.

Leaves rustled, a twig snapped.

* * *

"Has anyone seen Kate?" Holly said when they got back to the barn. Marcia and Laura were shampooing Soupçon in the wash stall, and the pony was trying to be a good sport about it.

Marcia blew a soap bubble off her nose. "She went looking for you."

"Soupy's all soapy," Laura sang as she hosed off her pony's hindquarters. He gave Holly a mournful look.

Get me out of here.

She'd never seen him so calm and cooperative. Normally, Soupy was a bundle of energy, barely able to stand still. Maybe the girls had washed it all out of him. Holly took off Magician's tack, rubbed him down, and tried not to worry about Kate.

Tapestry's stall was accusingly empty. Magician poked his nose over the partition and let out a deep, rumbling sigh, making Holly feel even more guilty about riding with Twiggy and Meredith. But Kate had been such a downer last night that Holly had wanted to get away—on her own. Running into Twiggy and Meredith in the barn earlier had been an unexpected bonus.

Just what she'd needed.

Twiggy's flushed face popped over Magician's door. "Let's go swimming."

"At the club?"

Frantically, Kate looked around, scared of what she might find and even more scared of what she wouldn. She scanned the woods and almost missed it—a pair enormous brown eyes looking straight at her from behind a low bush about twenty feet away.

"Oh, wow," she breathed. "It's a deer."

Motionless, the buck stared at her like a trophy on hunter's wall. Then, with a wave of his magnificent antlers, he took off, leaping over rocks and dodging around trees until his tawny brown body blended into the background and disappeared.

"Oh, wow," Kate said again.

Her hands trembled, her legs felt like jelly. She'd never seen a deer that big before. Would it survive the next hunting season? Lost in thought, Kate headed for the farm Surprisingly, there was nobody around. No noise, workmen bustling about, and no Sam Callahan pacing new property or conferring with a builder about how modernize the barn.

Kate had expected *some* signs of life—a couple of rabbits or even a flock of crows—but this was eerily Instead of the yellow backhoe, an old-fashioned tractor with enormous wheels now stood in the driv Perched jauntily on its metal seat was a red baseba Somehow, this small patch of color made Weath Farm seem a little less forlorn.

"No, silly. Your place," Twiggy said. "I hate the club's pool. They spray you with disinfectant before you go in."

"Do not," Holly said, laughing.

"Close enough," Twiggy said. "Come on. I'm hotter than a fried egg."

"Go on ahead," Holly said. "I'll catch up."

She pulled out her phone and texted Kate. She wouldn't get it on the mountain because cell service was spotty there, but hopefully she'd see it when she got close to the barn.

We're in the pool. Hurry home and jump in.

The message was kind of dumb, but it would have to do. With luck, it would stop her and Kate from spiraling out of control like the last time they'd gotten on each other's nerves. Holly sighed. This stepsisters thing was a lot more complicated than she'd expected. No, not *step-*sisters.

Sisters.

They'd both agreed on that.

* * *

The sweet aroma of shampoo hit Kate the minute she led Tapestry into the barn. It even overpowered the smell of manure. Telltale bubbles lingered in the wash stall. Soupy's wet halter dangled from a crosstie; giggles erupted from his stall.

Kate peeked inside.

Pink ribbons sprouted along the pony's bristly mane, his hooves sparkled, and swirls of rainbow glitter dotted his ample rump. A lopsided silver horn jutted between his ears like a party hat.

"He's a unicorn," Kate said.

Laura grinned. "No, he's a *pony*corn."

"We're practicing for Halloween," Marcia added.

"That's not for another three months," Kate said, trying to keep a straight face. For a moment, these two little girls and their long-suffering pony made her forget about being upset with Holly.

"Two and three-quarter months," Laura corrected.

"Ten weeks and six days," Marcia explained. "We counted." She nudged Laura. "And we're gonna win the contest."

"What contest?"

"The fancy dress contest," Laura said. "Didn't you hear?"

"No," Kate said. "Where?"

"At the Labor Day Show." Marcia rolled her eyes as if Kate were too stupid to live. "*Every*one's going to enter."

"Even Mrs. Dean?"

The words were out before Kate could stop them. But Angela's mother *would* make a perfect witch. She wouldn't need any makeup, either. Or a costume—she

for Kate's help at the museum. So far this week she'd only worked two hours, so she really owed him.

Like big time.

After giving Tapestry another round of kisses, Kate dropped off her tack and detoured into Liz's office to return the spurs she'd borrowed but hadn't used. Instinctively, she checked the white board.

Team lesson, 4:00 pm. DON'T BE LATE!

Her heart sank. If things went the way they normally did at the museum, she'd be lucky to get out by five. This meant she'd miss another practice. But Liz would understand. She was married to Dad. She knew about his deal with Kate.

Quickly, she scribbled a note to Liz and stuck it on the white board, then raced outside and pulled her bike from the rack. Seven minutes left. She'd make it in plenty of time.

* * *

While Twiggy and Meredith lazed about on the patio, Holly swam laps. She loved swimming almost as much as she loved riding. It had kept her from going nuts when she was stuck in a wheelchair and unable to walk. It had also made her strong.

At the deep end, Holly did an expert flip turn and

launched into her favorite stroke, the butterfly. Back and forth she went, churning through the water like a dolphin and wondering why Kate hadn't shown up. Had she ignored Holly's text?

Or had she missed it?

For a teen, Kate was surprisingly hopeless with cell phones, like she was with boys. It wouldn't be the first time their signals had crossed. Holly ramped up her speed and did four blistering lengths of the freestyle before climbing out of the pool. Silently, she crept up behind Twiggy and shook out her wet hair.

"Ooh, lovely," Twiggy said, shivering. "I was about to melt."

Holly plucked her cell off the picnic table. Nope, nothing from Kate. The others hadn't heard anything, either.

"Maybe she got lost," Twiggy said.

"Hardly," Holly replied, toweling herself off. "Kate knows the mountain almost as well as I do." She thought for a minute. "Besides, Tapestry would bring her home."

"Unless they got eaten."

"By what?"

Twiggy rolled her eyes. "The *coy-O-te*."

"Don't be silly," Meredith said, laughing. "This isn't *Little Red Riding Hood*."

"Or the wolf." Holly bared her teeth.

But despite the fun, she began to worry. It wasn't like Kate to go off on her own. Suppose Tapestry heard or saw the coyote and freaked out. Kate could be lying on the trail with a broken leg or a concussion. She'd be easy prey for a coyote. They rarely approached humans, unless—

Rabies.

No, this was stupid, utterly stupid. She'd be seeing pink elephants next. But, to be absolutely sure, Holly threw on a t-shirt and raced barefoot across the back field, straight into the barn. To her surprise, Angela was brushing Ragtime. He stuck his handsome head over the door and frisked Holly for treats.

She patted his nose. "Have you seen Kate?"

"No, why?" Angela replied. "Did you lose her?"

"Oh, never mind," Holly said.

Wishing she'd worn shoes, Holly picked her way carefully down the aisle and headed for Magician's stall. To her relief, Tapestry was happily nuzzling Magician's mane over their shared partition. Okay, so where was Kate and why hadn't she called?

Maybe she'd left a note.

Holly checked her mother's office. No message taped to Mom's chair or scribbled on the white board, and nothing on the floor except the usual mess. Assuming there *was* a note, where else would Kate have left it?

The tack room?

Holly found Tapestry's saddle on its peg with her bridle hanging below and Kate's grooming box on the floor beneath. She pulled out a curry comb and two brushes but didn't find a note tucked in there either. Her relief turned into irritation.

Kate wasn't in trouble.

At least, not in the woods, but she'd be in big trouble with Mom if she didn't get back in time for the lesson. Missing one was bad enough, but two in a row? It was enough to get Kate suspended from the team—unless she had a bulletproof excuse.

Puzzled and annoyed, Holly trudged home. It was almost three o'clock. Time to change back into her riding clothes.

6

TWIGGY DID HER BEST to pay attention to Liz's lesson, but her mind kept wandering. All she could think about was Diamond. Was he missing her? Did the grooms at Beaumont Park remember that his favorite snack was watermelon rinds?

"Inside rein," Liz yelled. "Outside leg."

So, of course, Twiggy got them muddled up, and poor Rebel ended up like a pretzel, cantering on the wrong lead. At the next corner, she straightened him out. It wasn't easy, riding another girl's horse. Rebel twitched his ears.

Are we done yet?

He was famous around the barn for loving vanilla pudding. The younger kids spoiled him rotten with sugary treats that he inhaled like a vacuum cleaner. Twiggy patted Rebel's neck as Holly trotted up beside her.

"Are you okay?"

"Yeah," Twiggy said, even though she wasn't. Her legs were about to fall off, and she wasn't sure her arms would stay attached to her body, either.

Holly grinned. "Mom can be tough."

"I know," Twiggy said, eyeing the gymnastic that Liz had just set up.

"But she's cool," Holly added.

Too stiff to argue, Twiggy took her turn over the jumps—an easy crossrail, two oxers, and a set of parallel bars that Rebel cleared with ease. Liz raised them all.

"You first," she said to Angela.

Ragtime tucked his front legs and bounded over the colorful jumps like a pro—which he was. Mrs. Dean had spent a fortune on this horse and it showed. Even Angela's careless riding didn't throw him off balance.

Kristina and Cody went next, followed by Robin on Chantilly. Then came Holly with Magician. Her black gelding soared over the fences as if they were no bigger than the toy jumps in Twiggy's bedroom back home. Rebel had no trouble with them, either, and Twiggy couldn't have been more thrilled. If everyone, including her, re-peated these performances on Monday for Meredith, she'd have a hard time choosing the final team.

Oh, except for Kate.

Holly hadn't said, but Twiggy knew she was worried or even angry that her sister hadn't shown up.

* * *

The post office line was taking for ever. Kate looked at her watch. Almost four thirty. If she hurried, she could make it back up the hill, saddle Tapestry, and be at Liz's riding team lesson before it ended.

Maybe.

Her box grew heavier by the minute, which was totally insane. Like, really, how much could a carton of butterfly babies weigh? Dad had packed it with peanuts and bubble wrap and whatever life-support systems the cocoons needed. Kate had no clue. As far as she was concerned, they were already shriveled up. Lifeless . . . waiting for something to set them off again, like the old woman in front of her.

"How much for a stamp?" she asked.

"Forty-nine cents," said the desk clerk.

But the woman wasn't convinced. What if she bought a hundred? Wouldn't that get her a discount?

"No," said the desk clerk. "They're still forty-nine cents, no matter how many you buy."

They went back and forth, discussing the merits of buying a hundred stamps versus buying twenty, until Kate wanted to strangle the old woman. Didn't she realize there was a line of people behind her, arms loaded with packages and letters to mail?

Finally, the woman turned. Her leathery, wrinkled face

spoke of many years outside. She took in Kate's irritated expression and glanced down at her less-than-clean boots. "Nice," the woman said, nodding. "I used to ride, a long time ago." Her pale eyes grew wistful as if suddenly filled with old memories. "Do you have a horse?"

"Yes."

"What breed?"

Taken aback, Kate said, "She's a Morgan."

"What's her name?"

"Tapestry," Kate replied. "From Richard North's farm."

"Know it well," said the woman, leaning on her knobby cane. "Good horses. All of 'em."

Kate's impatience fizzled and drained away, right down her legs and out through the tips of her dusty riding boots the old woman had just admired.

"Who are you?" Kate blurted.

"Nobody you'd know," the woman said, and limped off. A man coming into the post office, held the door open for her.

Feeling humbled, Kate set her package on the counter. She paid the postage and went outside to collect her bike. For a few seconds, she stood perfectly still and looked up at Timber Ridge Mountain. It was all there—her life, her hopes, and her dreams. And if a mysterious old woman at the post office had delayed Kate from reaching them—just for a little bit—who cared?

They would always be there.

It was up to her to make it all happen—her riding, her skill with a horse. Kate jumped on her bike and pedaled up the hill, but when she got to the barn, the riding team lesson was already over.

Holly gave her a sour look. "You messed up."

* * *

No matter what Kate said, Holly didn't believe her about the note. It just wasn't there; it was all in Kate's head. She must have imagined writing it.

Kate finally gave up.

There was no sense trying to defend herself when Holly was in such a pissy mood. It happened all the time, and Kate knew better than to argue.

She slouched back to the house, made herself a sloppy egg salad sandwich, and collapsed on the living room couch. It no longer felt like home. Even Dad bursting through the back door didn't improve things, never mind that he thanked Kate all over again for helping at the museum.

"Couldn't have done it without you," he said. "I hope Liz won't be mad at me."

Holly said, "I saw a coyote."

"Where?" Kate said, thankful that Holly had changed the subject.

"In the woods. It was enormous."

"I'm not surprised," Dad said. "They have a lot to eat out there. Rabbits, squirrels, possums, and—"

"—people?" Holly said.

Dad burst out laughing. "Whatever gave you that idea?"

"Dunno," Holly said. She sat down beside Kate. Close, but not quite touching. "Something I read?"

"Well, whatever it was, it's wrong," Dad said, rubbing his salt-and-pepper beard. "Coyotes won't attack humans unless they're rabid, and even then, it's rare. But they've become a real menace for pets in urban areas."

"Where?"

"Boston, New York . . . all over the northeast," Dad said. "Some coyotes have lost all their fear of humans. They've gotten so bold that a couple of them actually jumped the fence into someone's backyard, snatched two dogs, and jumped out again."

Holly gasped. "No!"

"And," Kate said, "a woman in our old neighborhood was walking her poodle when a coyote shot out of the bushes and yanked her dog right off its leash."

"But why?" Holly said.

"Not enough wild critters for them to eat in a built-up area," Dad said, "so they're stealing pets." He looked at both girls. "If a coyote comes close, wave your arms and make a lot of noise. It usually scares them off."

"Hazing," Kate said.

"Oh, and by the way," Dad said to Holly. "That animal you saw probably wasn't a coyote, but a hybrid we call a coywolf."

"*Wolf?*"

"They've interbred," Dad said. "The coyotes and wolves. Dogs, too. It's the domestic canine's blood that makes the coywolf less afraid of humans."

"Yikes," Holly said, turning pale.

Kate had heard it all before. Get her father going on the subject of species, and he would talk all night. Or argue. It depended on his audience. While Holly asked questions, Kate thought about the huge deer she'd seen. That was probably what had been watching her on the trail, following her with his enormous brown eyes.

"I saw a deer," she said.

Holly shrugged. "They're all over the place."

Okay, that was clearly a nonstarter. Kate tried again. She offered Holly the other half of her sandwich.

"No, thanks. I'm not hungry."

This had to be a joke. Holly was *always* hungry, and she adored egg salad almost as much as she adored butter-crunch ice cream. There was a carton in the fridge. Kate shared it out, but Holly didn't want any ice cream, either. Dad ate her portion, then disappeared down the hall.

"Are you mad at me?" Kate said, the moment his office door banged shut.

"Yes."

"Why?" Kate hated pushing because it invariably backfired and made things even worse. But this time she wouldn't back down.

"First, because you blew me off, and—"

"How?"

"You didn't answer my text."

"I didn't even *see* it," Kate said. Dad's phone call had taken care of that. She'd never even thought to check for messages.

"*And*," Holly went on, sounding so righteous that Kate wanted to stick her fingers in both ears, "you didn't leave a note."

"But I did." Kate repeated what she'd already said. "On the white board. I taped it up—an orange one." Or was it red? At this point, she was too frazzled to remember.

"Okay," Holly said. "So, where is it?"

"Maybe it fell behind Liz's desk."

"I looked," Holly said. "It wasn't on the floor, either."

"How could you tell?" Liz's office wasn't the tidiest place on the planet. Half the time it looked worse than their bedroom. "Angela?" Kate finally said, grasping at straws. "I bet she took it down."

"Oh, get real," Holly snapped. "She's not dumb enough to pull the same trick twice."

Despite herself, Kate had to agree. It would be incredibly dumb, but right now it was the only answer that made sense. Last year Angela had not only messed with Liz's white board like she had yesterday, but she'd also trashed several notes that Kate had left for Liz. Why didn't Holly get this? Kate wanted to ask, but Holly's frosty expression stopped her cold.

Time to back off and think.

This was totally ridiculous, arguing about a stupid note. And why was Holly defending Angela? Was it because of Twiggy? Kate banished the thought, but it kept worming its way into her mind as the evening wore on. Holly had a "She's mine because I met her first" attitude about the princess, almost as if she didn't want Kate to be part of their cozy little circle.

Holly, Twiggy, and Angela?

Hello?

That was even more ridiculous. Twiggy couldn't stand Angela. She'd made that quite clear, but she was the Deans' guest and had to be polite. Given half a chance she'd move in with Kate and Holly except there wasn't room. Not for her *and* a bodyguard.

Meredith?

Where did she fit in? Was she part of their inner circle, too? Kate was still wrestling with this when Liz came home, told Kate that she understood about the mix-up and that Kate was still on the team. "Next time," she said, finishing off the carton of buttercrunch, "don't leave a note. Text me instead."

"Yeah, okay, and thanks," Kate said, though texting Liz was like shooting words into a black hole. They went in but rarely came out the other end. Most of the time her stepmother's cell phone was elsewhere, like on the kitchen counter or in her truck while Liz was in the barn.

Feeling miserable, Kate changed in the bathroom and climbed into bed. Holly was already asleep, or pretending to be, with an armful of stuffed ponies.

Kate turned off her light.

This was going to be a difficult weekend. No, make that a difficult week . . . or even longer.

7

IT WAS BARELY LIGHT when Holly got up, much earlier than normal. She microwaved a mug of last night's coffee and took a cautious sip.

"Yikes!"

Way too hot. Holly poured it down the drain. Okay, so what about cereal or fried eggs? She felt hollow inside but couldn't face real food. Instead, she grabbed a candy bar for later, slipped into her boots, and left for the barn before anyone else was awake. Even the horses were still yawning when she tossed flakes of hay into their stalls.

Magician and Tapestry had spent the night in the back paddock. Holly led them inside, measured out grain and supplements, and topped up all the water buckets. Then she trundled back outside with hay for Marmalade and the ponies.

Ground mist drifted like feathers around their legs; trees and shrubs took on ghostly shapes. The weathervane creaked. Everything was soft and muted as dawn's deep purple, indigo, and pale mauve ran together like a water-color left out in the rain. For a moment or two, Holly stood quietly, taking it all in. She loved mornings like this. Just her and the horses, watching the sunrise, and—

A movement caught her eye.

Up came Marmalade's enormous head, bits of hay sticking out of his mouth like a scarecrow. Daisy pinned her ears and threatened to kick Snowball. Even Plug abandoned his breakfast. Tails flagged, the ponies took off, squealing and bucking and racing around the paddock with Marmalade lumbering behind them.

Holly froze. The hairs on the back of her neck stood up. She'd heard of this happening to others, but she had always laughed it off as a myth.

Not any more.

Those hairs really were standing up. Heart thumping hard enough to leap out of her mouth, Holly didn't know whether to stay perfectly still or race back into the barn.

Was it a coyote?

Didn't Ben say to jump up and down and wave your arms? What if you couldn't actually see it? But Holly knew it was there. She could feel it. The ponies did, too. They were still snorting and freaking out.

Now what?

Would the horses chase it off? They were four against one, and they had teeth and hooves. Holly had nothing except herself.

Slowly, she backed away—holding her breath and not daring to turn—until she reached the barn. It wouldn't follow her inside, would it? She slammed the door behind her. A ginger cat erupted from an empty stall, yowling.

"Don't go outside," Holly cried.

Claws extended, the cat dodged around her and leaped through an open window. Watching it go, Holly was glad they'd never named the barn cats. When they finally disappeared, it was easier to forget about them if they didn't have cute names like Fluffy or Socks or Patches.

Holly gulped.

With luck, the cat would climb onto the roof or scamper up a tree. The side door creaked open, and Holly jumped as light spilled into the barn. Twiggy stepped inside. Behind her came Angela and Meredith, all three of them backlit by the early morning sun. Dizzy and half-blinded, Holly put a hand to her face. Despite the heat, she felt cold and clammy, as if she were about to pass out.

"You look awful," Twiggy said, running toward her. "Did you just see a ghost?"

"No," Holly whispered. "I —"

All of a sudden, she couldn't find the words. They

were right there, on the tip of her tongue, but none of them made any sense. Slowly, the barn tilted sideways, her legs buckled, and the floor rushed up to meet her.

* * *

Kate was halfway to the barn when her cell phone buzzed. "Holly fainted," Meredith said. "I called an ambulance."

Heart beating fast, Kate ran the rest of the way and arrived to find Holly sitting on the barn floor, head down, and breathing into a brown paper bag.

"In and out," Meredith said. "Slowly."

"Are you all right?" Kate said, kneeling beside her sister.

Was this another panic attack? Holly was the strongest person Kate knew, but her tough-girl façade had been shattered two weeks ago when a troubled girl from Holly's past had stalked her on Facebook. It was totally scary, but Kate had managed to help Holly through it.

Would it work this time?

Vaguely, Kate registered Twiggy and Angela, hovering in the background and looking scared. Holly's face was so pale you could almost see through it. In the distance, a siren wailed getting closer and closer. Holly struggled to get up.

Gently, Meredith pushed her down. "Keep breathing."

Two medics ran through the door. One placed an oxygen mask over Holly's nose; the other medic, much younger, took her pulse and blood pressure. Holly's stomach gurgled like water going down a drain. The first medic, whose nametag said Wendell, frowned and looked at Kate.

"When's the last time she ate?"

Holly tried to rip her mask off. "I'm—"

"Take it easy," the young medic said, pumping up the pressure cuff again. He looked barely old enough for his job.

"I don't know," Kate said.

Last night, Holly had refused the sandwich and ice cream, and when Kate had cruised through the kitchen just now, all she'd seen was an empty coffee mug in the sink. No toast crumbs on the counter, no dirty cereal bowl or half-eaten banana.

"Is she dieting?" Wendell said.

"No way," Kate said. Holly was a perfect size eight, and she never gained weight, no matter how much she scarfed down. The girls at school envied her.

"Does she have an eating disorder?"

Kate snorted. "She's addicted to egg salad and butter-crunch ice cream."

"Together?"

For some idiotic reason, it broke the ice. Kate said, "My sister eats like a horse."

Wendell removed the mask and helped Holly to sit up straighter. "Feeling better, now?"

"Yeah."

Just then, Angela ran up with an armload of fleece saddle pads and tucked them around Holly. This was almost more shocking than Holly passing out. Wendell pinched the skin on the back of her hand.

"She's dehydrated," he said. "Get some water."

Twiggy pulled a sports bottle from her knapsack. "Where's Liz?" she said, as Holly gulped it down.

"Did anyone call her?" Meredith said.

"I did," Angela replied. "She's on her way."

Surprise number two. Was Angela turning over a new leaf? "Thanks," Kate said, feeling embarrassed for not doing it herself. Of course, *Liz*.

Like, duh-uh, Holly's *mother*.

She blew into the barn five seconds later. "What happened?"

Kate moved over to give Liz more room. She must've gotten dressed in a blazing rush—mismatched sneakers, one sock, and a green polo shirt, inside out.

They exchanged a quick glance, and Liz's worried expression reminded Kate why she'd been hired as Holly's watchdog last year. Liz had been convinced, with good reason, that her headstrong daughter would attempt something monumentally dumb, like barreling down stone steps in her wheelchair, or that she'd disobey orders and swim on her own. Thanks to hours of swimming, Holly had strong shoulders, but they hadn't been strong enough to haul herself out of a pool without help.

And Liz had been right.

On the day of her interview, Kate had arrived early and pulled an exhausted Holly up the pool's ladder before her mother got home. It pretty much sealed their friendship. They'd been rescuing each other from scrapes ever since.

Wendell said, "She's all right, ma'am. Just hungry."

"That's nothing new," Liz said, sounding relieved. "Holly is *always* hungry."

"Except she hasn't eaten," Kate said. Holly would probably kill her for butting in, but somebody had to. "Not since yesterday morning."

"Is this true, young lady?" Wendell said, and Kate winced because Holly hated being called *young lady*. They all did. Guys like him ought to know that.

Holly rolled her eyes.

"That's enough," Liz said. She gave Holly a quick hug. "I don't know what's gotten into you, but you're going straight back home. You will eat food—*real* food—and you're not riding today."

"But, *Mom*," Holly wailed, "I saw a coyote out there."

"You were hallucinating," her mother said. "That's what happens when you're half starving. Now, come on."

Liz got to her feet and hauled Holly up with her. She looked at Kate. "You take her. I've got a lesson in ten minutes."

Meredith stepped forward. "I'll do it. I probably shouldn't be riding, either." She glanced at Twiggy. "And neither should you. Not without me. No going on the trails, okay? Just the ring."

"Okaaaay," Twiggy said.

The walkie-talkie strapped to Wendell's belt sprang into life. Turning away, he answered, while the other medic gathered up their equipment.

"We've gotta run," Wendell said. "A guy just fell off his roof."

"What was he doing up there?" Liz said.

"Rescuing his cat, apparently."

Sirens wailing, the ambulance left even faster than it had arrived. Kate hoped the guy would be okay. His cat, too.

* * *

Perched on the sawhorse in Liz's office, Kate watched her new stepmother rummage through papers and files on her messy desk.

Stepmother?

It brought up visions of *Cinderella* and the wicked queen from *Snow White*. Stepmothers in fairy tales definitely got a bad rap. But what about real life? Apart from

Marcia Dean, Kate had never met anyone with a step-mother before.

Right after the wedding, Liz had said, "What do you want to call me?"

"What's wrong with Liz?" Holly had chimed in. "It's what I'm going to call Kate's dad."

"Really?" Ben had said.

They'd all laughed, but it made Kate think of her own mother. How would she feel about Kate calling someone else *Mom*? She'd probably be fine because she wanted Ben to be happy and Kate to have a loving family.

But in the end, Kate had settled for Liz. It was more comfortable, and it was what she'd called Holly's mom ever since arriving at Timber Ridge. Until then, Kate had never called a grownup by her first name before, not even her old riding instructor, Mrs. Mueller.

"It's my fault," Kate now said morosely.

"What is?"

"Holly, not eating."

Without looking up, Liz said, "Since when are you in charge of my daughter's stomach?" From beneath an old tack catalog, she pulled out the spurs Kate had returned yesterday. "Ah, here they are. Now, stop beating yourself up, Kate. You are not to blame. Holly's a big girl. If she forgets to eat dinner or breakfast or whatever, it's her fault, not yours."

"Yeah, but—"

"Look, I know you guys have been snipping at one another lately. I have no idea why, and it's not my business. But you'll get over it. You always do." Liz gave an odd little smile. "I snipped at your father last night."

"You did?" Kate wanted to ask why but didn't dare.

Liz said, "Ben complained when I jacked up the air conditioner. Heat doesn't bother him. He could wear a fur coat in a sauna and not break a sweat."

"That's because he spent years in the jungle." Kate caught her breath, remembering all the birthdays and holidays her father had missed because he was in Brazil or Borneo chasing rare butterflies and moths. "Mom had the same problem with him."

There was an awkward silence.

"Thanks for telling me," Liz said, twisting her gold wedding ring. "It means a lot."

One of the adult boarders poked her head around Liz's door. She wore blue breeches, a dark blue helmet, and a blue-checked shirt. "Are you ready for us?"

Behind her stood a blue roan gelding that matched her outfit, more or less. His saddle pad and leg wraps were the exact same check as his rider's shirt. Even his bell boots were blue.

Holly would love it.

Had she really seen a coyote by the back paddock, or had she been hallucinating like Liz said? Thanks to Dad,

Kate knew quite a bit about wildlife, and coyotes in particular. But these coywolves were a menace. Apparently, a pack of them had injured a horse in Minnesota so badly that it had to be put down.

Kate shuddered, then glanced at Liz's white board. *Team lesson at five.* This time, she would *not* miss it.

* * *

Angela had Ragtime on the crossties. Playfully, he nudged Kate as she ducked beneath his lead rope.

"Sorry, no treats," she said.

"He's already had plenty," Angela said, brushing Ragtime's neatly pulled mane.

Kate gaped like a goldfish.

Was this really Angela, taking care of her own horse without grumbling that it was too much work? Ragtime's saddle and bridle were propped on a tack trunk, and it was obvious that Angela had groomed Ragtime far better than she normally did. His mahogany coat positively gleamed. She'd even slopped polish onto his hooves.

So, who was she trying to impress?

"Don't tell Meredith, but I'm going for a trail ride with Angela," Twiggy called out from Rebel's stall. "Wanna come with us?"

"Yeah, I guess," Kate said, feeling awkward.

This wouldn't be the first time Twiggy had disobeyed

her father, and it probably wouldn't be the last. But that was Twiggy's problem, not Kate's. She had enough problems of her own.

Never mind what Liz told her, Kate still felt guilty. Last night, her fight with Holly had reached the silly stage when Holly made a big deal out of turning down Kate's sandwich, followed by scorning her favorite buttercrunch ice cream.

Holly had refused to back down.

She was obviously hungry but wouldn't admit it because that would've meant losing face in front of Kate. She was funny like that.

As for breakfast?

Even though Kate knew it was the most important meal of the day, she often skipped it. Sometimes you were in too much of a hurry to hit the barn before anyone else.

It didn't take long to get Tapestry ready. For once, she hadn't rolled in the dirt. Kate began to cheer up. Without Holly around, it would be a good chance to get to know Twiggy better—unless Angela hogged all her attention.

Angela?

What was she up to this time?

8

Twiggy had a list. She wanted to see the lake, the cross-country course, the hermit's old house where Kate had found Tapestry, and Sam Callahan's new barn.

Kate frowned. "That'll take all day."

"We've got till three," Angela pointed out. "Then we come back to the barn, give the horses a rest, and be ready for our lesson at five."

"I've even brought lunch," Twiggy said.

Well, not exactly lunch. More like yummy snacks. Her knapsack bulged with chocolate chip cookies, peanut butter treats, and English Mars Bars—called Milky Ways over here. She had extra water bottles, too.

For a moment, she felt a bit guilty over lying to Meredith. But honestly, how much trouble could she get into?

This was Vermont, not a war zone. Besides, Dad would never find out.

And if he did?

No big deal. Meredith was taking another job, anyway. It wasn't as if he could fire her. But he could drag Twiggy home.

She'd worry about it later.

"I guess it'll be okay," Kate said, "as long as we take it easy. We don't want to tire the horses out."

Without any effort, she vaulted into Tapestry's saddle. Twiggy wished *she* could do that. Kate made it look easy—you just bounced a couple of times and up you went, like vaulting on the pommel horse at school which Twiggy had never been able to learn. Her arms and legs had refused to cooperate when it came to gymnastics.

Maybe Kate would teach her.

Twiggy added "vaulting" to her American bucket list. At the rate it was growing, she'd never get through it by the end of August. She still hadn't been to New York and gone to the top of the Empire State Building or seen the Statue of Liberty.

The Grand Canyon?

No, silly, that wasn't around here. Twiggy sighed. This country was so amazingly huge that you couldn't see it all in twenty minutes like you could England. Well, maybe not *quite* that fast, but—

Rebel dodged sideways.

Twiggy landed halfway up his neck. Her fault. She'd been lollygagging around, not paying attention. Feeling like a nitwit, she got herself upright again. It was just an old tree stump he'd shied at.

Twenty minutes later they reached Crescent Lake. Families picnicked on the beach; kids splashed each other and dived off the raft. One landed in a huge, inflatable dinosaur. His buddy tried to duck him.

Sweat trickled down Twiggy's face.

If only she'd worn her bathing suit. It would be such fun to ride a horse into the water. She'd only done it once when Holly and Kate and a guy from Holland, who was really cute, had rescued her on horseback from an island in Cornwall.

It had all been very exciting—even if she couldn't remember half of it—and on top of that she'd met Nathan Crane. They were now dating—well, sort of. Nathan had blown through Winfield last week in his fancy new car, they'd shared a pizza, and then he'd swanned off to Romania (or was it New Zealand?) to begin shooting the sequel to *Moonlight*, her favorite movie ever. Dad hadn't approved. He said Nathan was only interested in Twiggy because she was a princess.

Kate had disagreed. "No way. Nathan really likes you."

And Kate ought to know. She'd once dated him herself.

* * *

The trail wasn't wide enough to ride three abreast, so Kate suggested they ride side-by-side and swap places every ten minutes or so. Angela graciously gave up her spot beside Twiggy.

"Your turn for the princess," she said, plugging in her earbuds.

"Thanks," Kate said.

It was really weird, seeing Angela like this. The last time she'd acted like an ordinary kid was at the Festival of Horses in April. Her old horse, Skywalker, had been at the show with his new owner, and Kate had found Angela crying.

In a moment of gut-wrenching honesty, Angela had tearfully admitted that she missed Skywalker like mad, that she'd never dared get close to one of her horses because the minute she did, her mother would sell it and buy a better one, like she had with Angela's first pony that she'd taught to bow and shake hands.

Kate had melted.

She'd actually hugged her rival. For those few precious minutes, they'd just been two girls who loved horses. But Angela had stiffened. She'd pulled back and muttered something about her mother, and the moment had vanished.

Mrs. Dean.

No wonder Angela had such a hard time fitting in and making friends—unlike Twiggy whose overprotective father was just as difficult as Mrs. Dean. But, despite Prince Ferdinand and his idiotic demands, Twiggy had made friends all over the place.

She said, "Kate, I love your horse."

"Thanks," Kate said. "I kinda love her, too."

"What's her favorite treat?"

"Carrots."

"Diamond goes nuts over watermelon rinds," Twiggy said. "Can you believe it?"

"Yes." Kate took a chance and told Twiggy about Black Magic and how she'd been blamed for his death. His favorite treats had been watermelon rinds, too. Most of Kate's t-shirts back then were stained pink.

"Eek," Twiggy said. "That must've been totally awful. You were *so* brave. I'd have freaked out."

This was part of Twiggy's charm. She spewed genuine sympathy like a fountain and often made it funny.

Was it an act? Had she been trained to do this? Her concern could be nothing more than a knee-jerk reaction to years of royal brainwashing. Kate had no idea.

Behind them, Angela was ambling along, listening to her iPod and snapping her fingers, just like a regular teen. Maybe all she needed was a chance—and a different mother.

There was a break in the trees, and Timber Ridge

Mountain towered above them. Ski trails, still vibrant with summer grass, spilled from its peak like dribbles of green paint. Kate had learned to ski last winter and couldn't wait to try it again this season.

"Can you ski?" Twiggy said.

"Yes," Kate said. "But not very well."

With a laugh, Twiggy launched into scary tales of skiing in Austria and Switzerland. "I took a wrong turn and went down an Olympic slope by mistake."

"Seriously?"

"Yeah, it was awesome," Twiggy said.

Kate wasn't surprised. When it came to danger, the princess gobbled it up like candy. She'd been totally unfazed about being kidnapped in London and had treated the whole thing as a huge joke. But her bravado took a sudden U-turn when Kate showed her the cross-country course.

"No way," Twiggy said. "Those fences are huge."

"Rebel can jump them," Angela said. "No problem."

"Not with me," Twiggy said.

Kate was impressed. Twiggy seemed to know her boundaries no matter how off-the-wall she sometimes behaved. A hundred yards farther on, their trail crossed a wide, gentle slope. Up one side marched a line of lift towers festooned with candy colored cable cars taking summer visitors to the summit for magnificent views across three states.

"Can we do that?" Twiggy said.

"Sure," Kate said. "But after the show."

"Cool," Twiggy said. "One more thing for my list."

Rebel arched his neck and looked warily at a yellow-and-black sign that said "Danger."

"He's fooling you," Kate said.

With the merest hint of her hands, she guided Tapestry toward the trail that led to the old man's cabin. Would Tapestry remember it and get upset? They hadn't ridden this way since last year when Kate had rescued Magician and seen Tapestry for the first time.

Old memories flooded back—her beloved horse, starved and neglected in a field littered with junk tires, abandoned trucks, and scraggly chickens that pecked at Tapestry's legs. No wonder she hated them.

The shack was abandoned—no smoke curling from its lopsided chimney, no crazy hermit staggering onto his tumbledown front porch and threatening them with a gun.

"So, where is he?" Twiggy said, looking around.

"I don't know," Kate said, relieved the old man was no longer there. Maybe he'd been put into a retirement home. She hoped he was safe and being taken care of. But Twiggy seemed disappointed, as if she'd expected outlaws or a shoot-out like an old cowboy film.

"I'm hungry," Angela said.

They found a grassy spot, got off their horses, and pawed through Twiggy's knapsack. Kate bit into a Mars

Bar and remembered how much she'd loved them in England. Angela scarfed up the cookies while Twiggy dug into her peanut butter treats. It was all very sugary. They'd be flying high later. Kate reminded herself to eat lots of vegetables with dinner.

"What time is it?" Twiggy said.

Kate checked her cell phone. No service, but that was normal for this part of the mountain. "Two fifteen. We should be getting back." The weather wasn't looking too good either. It was humid and oppressive, the kind of heat that often gave way to sudden storms.

"No," Twiggy said. "I want to see Mr. Callahan's farm."

From here, it was a minor detour, so Kate figured that if they didn't dawdle, they could make it home by three o'clock. She hoisted herself into Tapestry's saddle. Up ahead, the trail forked. Kate took a left, toward the Callahan's dirt road, and kept a lookout for deer. It would be so cool to see that buck again.

* * *

Twiggy took her turn bringing up the rear. She grew farther and farther behind because she kept stopping, hoping to catch sight of that coyote again. This time she would take a picture of it.

But all she saw were squirrels and a large raccoon eyeing her from a tree. She'd never seen one before, at least not outside of a zoo. Raccoons weren't native to England; neither were skunks. Last night, Twiggy had smelled one for the first time.

Ewwwww!

Worse than rotten eggs. The footing grew more rocky, and Rebel stumbled. Alarmed, Twiggy jumped off, lifted his front leg, and broke a fingernail picking stones from his hoof. By the time she remounted, Kate and Angela were out of sight. No problem. She could easily catch up. But around the next corner was yet another fork.

Okay, which way had they gone?

She'd let Rebel decide. He could probably hear the others. Horses had good ears, didn't they?

Without hesitation, Rebel turned right. He wasn't limping, either, thank goodness. The trail narrowed; it twisted and turned. Twiggy ducked to avoid a low-hanging branch, then stopped to remove a bramble that had gotten itself tangled in Rebel's mane. Still no sign of the others.

Had she taken a wrong turn?

Another raccoon popped up, a lot closer. Twiggy yanked her phone out so fast, it squirted through her fingers like a bar of wet soap.

Oh, great.

With an exasperated sigh, Twiggy slid off Rebel again. Her phone had wedged itself between two rocks. She hooked Rebel's reins over one arm and tried to pry the phone loose. Was it broken? She shouldn't have taken off its cover, but the stupid phone wouldn't fit into her pocket unless—

Rebel snorted. He tugged at his reins so hard that Twiggy almost let go. *Darn it.* She'd just gotten a grasp on her phone, too. It really was jammed. How on earth did something fall, land between two rocks, and get so stuck you couldn't pry it out? What she needed was a knife.

Was it still in her knapsack?

Twiggy eased it off her shoulders and was searching for the Swiss Army knife Dad had given her last Christmas, when Rebel snorted again. This time he jerked so violently, his reins broke.

She grabbed for them, but missed.

Rebel took off, leaving her stranded in the woods with whatever it was that had freaked him out.

9

KATE AND ANGELA HAD JUST TURNED into Sam Callahan's dirt road when Rebel raced up, nostrils flaring and stirrups flying.

"Omigod," Angela said. "Where's Twiggy?"

Good question. Kate had been so focused on talking with Angela and trying not to put her foot in it that she hadn't bothered to look behind. She'd just assumed Twiggy was following them.

"My bad," Kate said.

Somehow, she managed to grab Rebel's reins and hand them over to Angela. Then she took off up the trail. Turning right, she tried to remember the last time she'd seen Twiggy. Five minutes ago? Ten?

She couldn't be far away.

Kate tried one trail after another. Twiggy had obviously gotten lost. Was she hurt? Kate's anxiety rose as she pushed her mare further into the woods. Everything began to look the same.

"Twiggy," she called.

No answer.

She tried again, louder. "TWIGGY . . . *where are you?*"

* * *

First, it was one shape, then two. Twiggy wasn't sure what she was seeing. They shifted positions, never quite showing themselves. She tried her cell phone again, but not only was the screen cracked, there was no service on the mountain.

Kate had warned her about this.

Feeling excited and scared all at once, Twiggy sat on a rock. Around her, leaves rustled and bushes trembled. Whatever was out there seemed to be coming at her from all directions.

Don't panic.

It was probably raccoons and squirrels. Twiggy racked her brain, trying to remember what she'd read about American wildlife, so different from that in England. There were snakes and possums and really evil things with sharp teeth and bad attitudes called fishercats.

And coyotes.

They wouldn't attack her, would they? No, silly.

They'd run away. They weren't aggressive like wolves. If her stupid phone wasn't busted, she could get some great pictures. But maybe it wasn't dead. She tried taking a shot of her foot.

Oh boy, it worked.

If only she had her Nikon and its fancy lenses. Her dream, which she never shared with anyone else, was to be a wildlife photographer and travel to remote parts of the world, like Bora Bora and the Antarctic. Dad would have a cow if he knew.

Twiggy deleted her foot.

Assuming that Rebel had found Kate and Angela, one of them would come back to find her. In the meantime, she would keep calm and be very patient—just like her idol, Sir David Attenborough.

He wasn't scared of anything.

In Africa, he'd crawled into a giant ants' nest and taken the most amazing photos, never mind that ants the size of Volkswagens were crawling all over him and biting, hard. Something moved, then melted into the woods.

Aim, click, click. Did she get it?

Oh, hello *National Geographic*!

* * *

Much to her disgust, Kate ended up retracing her steps— going in circles, really—and wound up back where she'd left Angela. Clearly, she didn't know these woods as well as she'd thought. If only her dumb cell phone worked. She tried Twiggy's number again but got nowhere.

"Didn't you *find* her?" Angela's voice had an edge. She sounded like her old self and practically flung Rebel's reins at Kate.

"Why don't *you* try?" Kate said.

Angela tightened Ragtime's girth and swung herself into his saddle. "Okay, I will."

Leading Rebel, Kate followed on Tapestry. Angela rarely rode the trails and didn't have a clue where she was going. In less than ten minutes, she was totally lost.

But Kate wasn't.

She knew this trail. It led back to Sam Callahan's barn from the other direction, but that wasn't where they wanted to go. At least, not till they found Twiggy. Even then, there wouldn't be time. Kate checked her watch. They had to get home, like right now, if they wanted to rest the horses and be ready for Liz's lesson.

Something yipped, halfway between a bark and a yowl. Kate had heard this sound before, but even so, it still sent shivers down her spine.

Angela halted. "What's that?"

"A coywolf," Kate said. That's what Holly had seen yesterday and probably this morning, as well.

"What?"

Catching up to Angela, Kate explained how wolves

and coyotes had interbred. "They're not dangerous. They're more scared of us than we are of them."

"So, what are they doing here?" Angela said, sounding annoyed, as if these animals had invaded her space rather than the other way around. Coyotes and wolves had lived in this part of Vermont far longer than people had.

"It's their home."

Better not tell Angela about the horse in Minnesota. That was probably a fluke, anyway. They passed the turning to Weathervane Farm, took another right, and Kate finally spotted Twiggy sitting cross-legged on a rock and staring at a clump of bushes.

Twiggy held up a hand. "Be quiet."

"Why?"

"Coyotes."

Among the trees, Kate caught a glimpse of gray shapes, tails extended, creeping closer and closer. Was Twiggy feeding them?

"No," Kate cried.

But Twiggy reached into her knapsack and tossed out bits of food—crumbs, a handful of broken crackers. This wasn't right. Coywolves wouldn't approach her, unless—

Rabies?

Trying to keep calm, Kate led Rebel toward Twiggy. In a flash, she jumped off Tapestry, cupped Twiggy's knee, and hoisted her into Rebel's saddle before she had a chance to object. The princess landed hard, like a sack of potatoes.

"You've wrecked it," she wailed.

The biggest coyote staggered and fell over. Its mate took a step toward them. Two more appeared out of nowhere. A pack. Bigger than coyotes, so definitely coywolves.

For a moment, Kate froze.

Common sense told her these animals weren't dangerous, that they wouldn't attack a human. But that big one looked kind of crazy, maybe even rabid. Would it follow them? Would the others? A single coywolf wasn't a threat, but a whole pack might be.

Best not to risk it.

They needed a place to hole up, like right now. The barn was too far away, but what about Sam Callahan's place? It was just down the trail.

"Let's go." Kate vaulted into Tapestry's saddle and took off.

The coywolves followed, mostly out of sight in the woods. This was definitely weird behavior. They kept pace with the girls cantering along the narrow trail—not too near and not too far, either. Just close enough to remind Kate that they were still there. She hung a left and barreled down the dirt road. Then a right into Sam Callahan's deserted driveway.

Nobody there.

Not even that old green tractor had been moved. The red baseball cap was still on its metal seat, jaunty as ever. Flinging herself off Tapestry, Kate tried the barn door. Rusting hinges complained; old wood creaked and shifted. After another mighty shove, everything gave way and the barn's double doors slid open to reveal less of a mess than Kate had expected.

Empty stalls, draped with cobwebs, lined both sides of the aisle. A grain room with wooden bins sat on the right; moldering bales of hay were stacked at the far end. Kate dug her heel into hard dirt—no rotting floorboards to worry about. She led Tapestry into the first stall, kicked the partition to make sure it was sturdy, then beckoned Twiggy and Angela to follow.

"Shut the door," Kate yelled.

Twiggy wrestled it closed. Daylight vanished and left them all in the barn's dusty gloom. Small things scurried down the aisle; birds twittered from the rafters. Kate wiped layers of grime off a window with her elbow and peeked outside. The coywolf pack had vanished, except for the big one that looked kind of sick. He was crouched beneath a bush, out by the gate.

"What now?" Twiggy said.

Kate sucked in her breath. "We wait."

But how long would it take? They could be stranded

for hours until that coywolf got fed up and left or somebody at the barn figured out they'd gone missing. And, to
make matters worse, she heard a rumble in the distance.

Thunder?

"I'm scared," Angela said.

"We'll be okay," Kate said, wishing she felt as confi-
dent as she sounded.

* * *

Twiggy's bodyguard was great company. She entertained
Holly with stories about life on the dressage circuit and
didn't seem the least bitter that it had once let her down.
But now, thanks to Sam Callahan, Meredith said she was
back on track and looking forward to her new job.

"But I'll miss Twiggy," she added. "That princess is
something else."

"Yeah," Holly said.

After lunch, Meredith suggested a board game, but
Holly couldn't concentrate. Had Twiggy disobeyed orders
again and gone trail riding with Kate? Had Angela joined
them? Were they laughing about Holly? That would really
be the pits. Bad enough she'd fainted, but having them
poke fun because she'd seen a coyote, or thought she had,
was even worse.

Ugh.

Okay, maybe she'd exaggerated—just a teeny bit. It
could've been a raccoon or a possum that had set the

ponies off or even a chipmunk. You never knew with horses. Last week, Magician had freaked out over a dragonfly.

Holly dived into the pool. She swam ten wickedly fast laps and got back out again, flexing her muscles as if to prove to herself how wrong Mom was. Plus, she'd eaten two boiled eggs, a salad, and half an orange. Oh, and that candy bar.

She felt absolutely fine—and restless.

"Scrabble?" Meredith said.

Holly sighed. That was the last thing she wanted. But refusing would be rude, so she dragged up a lawn chair and sat down, dripping water all over the board that Meredith had set up.

Letters blurred and ran together. Holly rubbed her eyes. She had C-O-Y, but nothing else remotely useful.

"It's a word, right?"

"Yes," Meredith said, then slapped down O-T-E and scored a double.

Double.

Rhymes with trouble.

The sun disappeared behind a cloud and Holly shivered. She felt herself blanch, like she had that morning, but this was more real, more visceral—something deep in her gut that she could actually put her finger on. She'd never been more sure of anything in her life. Kate and Twiggy were in trouble. Angela, too.

Big trouble.

She could almost see them, in a dark place, with something threatening them. Holly didn't know what or where, but—

This was insane.

She wasn't a whacko. She didn't believe in premonitions or things that went bump in the night. Scary movies were great to laugh at. Ghosts didn't exist, nor did zombies, vampires, and werewolves.

But coywolves did.

* * *

The sky darkened. Lightning flashed, thunder rumbled, and the wind blew so hard that Kate figured a couple of the tallest trees would fall over. But they held firm, popping upright like rubber ducks in a bath tub.

She peeked outside.

That big coywolf was still there, lying by the gate and looking half dead or pretending to be. Even so, it wasn't safe to leave the barn. Not with a storm like this. They'd have to wait it out. Overhead, something crashed.

Angela cringed. "What's that?"

"Branches," Kate said.

Or it could be shingles, exploding off the barn's roof. The horses paced their temporary stalls. Tapestry nuzzled Kate's hand. Rebel whinnied. Even the unflappable Ragtime was restless. They all needed reassuring.

"It's okay," Kate said, patting her mare.

Angela snorted. "Easy for you to say."

She moved closer to Kate, never mind she probably hated herself for doing it. Whatever moments of friendship had passed between them on the trail were long gone. Angela was back to normal.

It was almost comforting.

At least, Kate knew where she stood with Angela but not with coywolves or the storm. Best thing they could do was hunker down and wait. Sitting on a pile of musty old grain sacks, Twiggy dug into her knapsack.

"I've got half a Mars Bar, two cookies, and a bag of chips."

"Water?" Kate said.

Twiggy shook her head. "All gone."

"But I'm thirsty," Angela complained.

"So are the horses," Kate said.

Apart from a few sips at the lake, they hadn't had anything to drink since leaving the barn. She tried her cell phone again. Still no service. It was now four thirty. In half an hour, Liz would be wondering why three of her riders had failed to show up.

10

FOR ONCE, HOLLY STOPPED TO THINK. Rushing off like a mad thing would make Meredith suspicious. She had to be sneaky about this, like plug in her iPod or pretend to take a nap.

"I'm kind of tired," she said.

Meredith yawned. "Me, too."

Casually, Holly folded the Scrabble board and scooped up the letters. Two fell into the pool. She would fish them out later. Stretched out beneath the patio umbrella, Meredith finally dozed off. Holly hung about for a few more minutes, then swapped her bathing suit for shorts and a t-shirt.

No, that wouldn't do, not if she planned to go riding. So she changed into breeches and took off for the barn. Thunder rumbled, but it was far away, on the other side of Timber Ridge Mountain.

Okay, now what?

Saddle up Magician without Mom seeing her and go looking for Kate? But where to begin? She could be anywhere—the hunt course, the lake, or up past the old man's shack.

What about Weathervane Farm?

Maybe she'd taken Twiggy to see it. That actually made sense. Of course, Twiggy would be curious about where Meredith was going to work. Yes, that's probably where they'd gone.

And they'd gone without *her*.

The air left Holly's body in a whoosh. For a few seconds, she actually felt dizzy. She sucked in a deep breath, then another like she'd done that morning in the barn.

Cautiously, Holly prodded her imagination, but those scary images she'd had by the pool weren't there any more. No more silly warnings, no more impending doom. This wasn't about coyotes or an imagined danger; it was about her being jealous. She was burning up with it.

"I'm *jealous*."

"Really?" said a voice.

Oh, no! Had she said it out loud? Blushing worse than Kate, Holly whirled around. In front of her stood the last person she wanted to see—at least, not right now when she'd just made a monumental fool of herself.

"What are you doing here?" she blurted.

Luke Callahan shoved a lock of brown hair off his forehead. "Well, hello to you, too."

"Lines," Holly said, thinking fast. "I'm rehearsing for a play." Boy, was that the dumbest excuse, ever?

"*Othello*?" he said.

"Huh?"

"Jealousy," Luke said, shooting Holly his trademark grin that even the most breathless horse show commentators couldn't begin to describe. "The bard's green-eyed monster."

This was totally surreal. In the blink of an eye, Holly had gone from seeing zombies and werewolves to discussing Shakespeare with show jumping's hottest new superstar. Clearly, she was dreaming. In a few minutes, she'd wake up and have a good laugh about this with Kate.

But no, it wasn't a dream.

Parked at an angle near the gate stood a very real dark-blue truck. Hitched up behind it was a matching gooseneck trailer with gold lettering on the side—Weathervane Farm. Its ramp was down. Wisps of hay and fresh manure had spilled across the parking lot. No sign of a horse, though. Frowning, Holly glanced at the barn, then back at Luke.

"Are you okay?" he said.

"Yeah."

"You're Holly, right?"

"Yeah," she said again.

This wasn't exactly a riveting conversation—nothing that would blow Luke away. Holly tried again, but her words came out all wrong. "What are you doing here?"

"You already asked that."

"And you didn't reply," she said.

His eyes narrowed, and Holly couldn't make up her mind if they were blue or green. A bit of both?

He said, still smiling, "My sister. I just dropped her off."

Sister?

Oh, right. Charlotte. She'd been at horse camp last month with her Norwegian Fjord. What was its name? Summer something-or-other. It had a nickname, too.

"Elke," Luke said, as if he knew exactly what Holly was thinking. He flashed that incredible smile again. "Charlotte's staying with Laura and Marcia."

"Oh?" Holly said.

But why hadn't Mom told them? It wasn't like her to have kids and ponies show up at the barn without warning.

"It was last minute," Luke said.

Again, he'd figured things out before Holly had even wrapped her mind around them. Was he psychic? Maybe that was why he was so much in tune with his horse. They'd certainly won enough ribbons. Perhaps Luke was a horse whisperer.

"Like when?" Holly said.

"This morning," Luke replied. "My sister said she hated Larchwood and conned me into bringing her back here." He looked over Holly's shoulder as if expecting to see someone else. "Where's Kate? Is she around?"

"Yeah—um, no," Holly said.

"Pity," Luke said. "My kid sister thinks she walks on water."

A couple of large raindrops landed on Luke's nose. He rubbed them off and left a tiny smear of dirt. Holly wanted to reach out and wipe it off.

Really?

What *was* she thinking? She *had* a boyfriend. Luke Callahan was totally off limits. Besides, she'd already decided that he'd be perfect for Kate. He seemed to like her, too. At the hospital, when Holly had said good-bye to Luke after Meredith's accident, he'd told her to tell Kate, "Hi."

But had she?

Holly couldn't remember—not that Kate would care one way or the other. She didn't seem to have any interest in Luke Callahan at all.

He waved toward his truck. "I'm going to check out the new place. Wanna come with me?"

"Sure, okay," Holly said, kicking at a clump of dirt. She had nothing else to do except feel sorry for herself. But that wouldn't be so easy to pull off now that Luke was here. His smile really was amazing.

The sky darkened.

"Hurry," Luke said, racing for his rig. He uncoupled the trailer and flung open his passenger door. Holly climbed inside. She sank into soft leather as hailstones the size of gumballs hammered the truck's windshield.

Soft leather?

Looking around, Holly tried not to gape. Was this really a truck? It felt more like Mrs. Dean's luxurious Mercedes, with its neatly folded plaid blanket and matching water bottles. Luke snapped on his seat belt, hit a few buttons on the dashboard, and the familiar sounds of "Hey Nineteen" surrounded them.

"Is Steely Dan okay with you?"

Holly nodded, kind of stunned. Did Luke love old music as much as she did, or was it his extrasensory perception again? Whatever. It didn't matter. Holly settled back to enjoy herself as they drove through the storm toward Weathervane Farm.

* * *

"It won't last long," Kate said, cringing as hail bounced off the roof and slammed into the barn's windows. Luckily, none of windows was in a stall, otherwise they'd have to move the horses for fear of breaking glass.

"How do you know?" Angela said.

Kate didn't. Not really. She'd only been stuck in a hailstorm once before, and it had lasted less than five minutes.

This one looked to be going on much longer, as if the sky had a never-ending supply of tiny white balls.

"No worries," Twiggy said cheerfully. "We could be here all night." She didn't sound the least bit upset. As far as Kate could see, this was just another adventure the princess would add to her bucket list. She was either very brave or totally clueless.

Kate had no idea.

And right now it didn't matter. If Twiggy's upbeat attitude kept Angela from panicking, this was a plus. It wouldn't take much to set the horses off, either. They could always sense when their riders were the slightest bit nervous, never mind if they were in the saddle or huddled on the ground in the middle of a strange barn.

Like right now.

Stiffness crept up Kate's legs. She'd been crouching for what felt like hours but was probably only a few minutes. How long would the storm last? But more, important, how long would that rabid coywolf hang about?

The others, she didn't worry about. They were long gone and wouldn't come back. The woods were filled with plenty of small critters for them to eat. But rabid animals were unpredictable, and the last thing you wanted was to be bitten by one of them.

Twiggy scrambled to her feet. "I'm bored."

"Sit down," Kate said, grabbing her.

But Twiggy shook off her grasp. She ran toward a

small window high above the mountain of musty hay bales. Off to one side was another door that Kate had already managed to get open. It was now firmly closed again.

She got up and followed, clambering up behind the princess, because who knew what she would do next? The window, like all the others, was covered in layers of dust and grime. Twiggy rubbed a small hole.

"Oh, no."

"What?" Kate said.

"Bunnies," Twiggy said, whipping around so fast she almost tumbled off the hay bales.

Kate held Twiggy's arm. "Careful."

Still holding onto the princess, she peered out the tiny window. There, on the barn's weedy front lawn, were three brown rabbits, nibbling grass and not seeming to care two hoots about the storm or the dangerous eyes that were watching their every move, just the way Twiggy was.

"Stop," Kate warned. "Don't—"

But, too late. In a flash, the princess slid off the hay bales. She snatched an old grain sack off the floor, then whipped open the barn's side door and bolted outside before Kate could stop her. As if they didn't have enough to worry about, Twiggy was now determined to save a bunch of innocent rabbits.

Kate wanted to save them, too.

But not right now when hailstones were pounding the roof and—

Lightning lit up the sky.

Forking left and right, it zapped and dazzled like a laser. Thunder followed. So did Kate. She raced out of the barn faster than Twiggy had.

Okay, so where was she?

* * *

Seamlessly, Luke's sound system switched from Steely Dan to One Direction, and "What Makes You Beautiful?" poured out.

"Seriously?" Holly said, delighted.

Luke snapped his fingers. "They're good."

This song was old but destined to be a classic, along with the Beatles' "Hey Jude," Rod Stewart's "Maggie May," and the Bee Gees's songs that everyone her age loved to hate. Oh, and Ravel's "Bolero"—even more ancient than Mom and Kate's dad and Aunt Bea.

But, for Holly, it didn't matter how old songs or musicians were, as long as they had a good beat. She snapped her fingers along with Luke. Together, they sang One Direction's lyrics. He didn't know them as well as she did.

Big deal . . . and who cared?

This was more fun than enough, never mind that the windshield wipers were having a hard time keeping up with the storm. Wrapped in a cocoon of music and buttery soft leather, Holly watched trees and farms whizz past her window. A herd of cows, looking wet and miserable, sheltered beneath a makeshift shed. In a blur of black and white they were gone, too.

"Not long, now," Luke said.

His iPhone, perched on the dashboard in a holder, displayed their route.

"Cell service is pretty bad on the mountain," Holly said, and then added that it might be kind of hard to run a show barn without cell phones.

"No problem," he said, pulling onto a dirt track. "Dad's putting in a tower."

And a new road? Holly wondered as Luke's truck bumped over ruts the size of small waves. It would've been even worse if he'd been pulling a trailer loaded with horses. Holly looked around—crumbling stone walls on the left, old barn ahead on the right, just the way she remembered.

Nothing different, except . . .

There was Princess Twiggy, on her hands and knees, crawling across the grass toward a bunch of wild rabbits, with Kate right behind her.

11

TWIGGY HELD HER BREATH. Just a tiny bit closer and she could grab that rabbit. Kate wasn't going to like this, but Twiggy didn't care. All she wanted was to save these cute bunnies from being eaten.

The biggest one hopped forward.

He reminded her of Fluffet, her favorite stuffed toy. Fluffet was brownish-pink with lopsided ears, and he really listened when you told him your problems. He was still in her room, hidden in a box at the back of her closet because Mum had wanted to toss him out with the rest of Twiggy's old toys.

"Fluffet?" she whispered.

He was tantalizingly out of reach. Did he know about the coyote or whatever it was off in the bushes and staring at both of them with scary eyes?

Yes, scary.

Thanks to Kate, Twiggy had learned a bit more about coywolves. This wasn't a wildlife special on TV. She wasn't Sir David with a cameraman and a backup crew ready to bale her out if she got in trouble.

She couldn't back down, either, not after making a big deal about rushing out of the barn to save the rabbits, no matter what. Somehow, she would get on with it. She could even imagine the BBC newsflash: *Beloved English princess mauled by wild animals in American wilderness. Updates at ten.*

From the barn, came a shrill neigh. Then another. Then all three horses were neighing and banging their stalls at once.

Angela screamed, "Help!"

"Come on." Kate grabbed Twiggy's ankle and pulled.

Twiggy fended her off. "You go. I can handle this."

She wasn't about to abandon the bunnies, especially Fluffet. Scrunching her eyes against the rain, Twiggy watched Kate hesitate like she couldn't make up her mind. Help Twiggy or stop Angela and the horses from having a meltdown?

"Go," Twiggy said again.

Yes, she was being incredibly stubborn. She got that— she really did. But how could anyone *not* want to save the rabbits? That coywolf wouldn't come anywhere near them as long as she was there, keeping him at bay. Angela yelled again, sounding close to panic.

"I'll be right back," Kate said. She whirled around and raced for the barn, head bent against the pounding rain. At least she hadn't scared the rabbits off. They hadn't even noticed her. Too busy nibbling grass.

Ears perked, Fluffet gave a few hops.

The others followed. Were they totally oblivious? Didn't they see that coyote? He was well hidden, blending into the background like a combat soldier in camouflage.

Noses twitched, bunny whiskers quivered.

Good, maybe they smelled him. Right now the only thing Twiggy could smell were the peanut butter crackers she'd eaten for lunch and managed to smear on her shirt.

Slowly, carefully, she inched forward on her elbows and knees like a marine on maneuvers. Hailstones stung as they bounced off her bare arms and pinged her riding helmet. The bunnies kept on nibbling, ears flicking back and forth. They must have heard her. With ears that size, they could probably hear the traffic in New York.

The plastic sack was so wet it kept slipping from her grasp. In desperation, Twiggy thrust her arm inside, straight through a hole at the other end. Perfect. It gave her something to hang onto. It felt kind of scratchy, though, but the bunnies wouldn't care. She'd throw the sack over them. Maybe not all three at once, but if she just captured Fluffet, he could live at the barn in a cute little hutch, and—

Suddenly, the bushes moved. She caught a glimpse of yellow eyes, wide open jaws, and ferocious teeth.

Twiggy froze.

Maybe this *wasn't* such a hot idea. She was about to back off when the coywolf launched itself like a missile. With a shriek, Twiggy flung her sack at the bunnies.

* * *

Holly leaped out of Luke's truck before it stopped moving. Feet skidding on wet grass, she took a bad step and crashed into Twiggy, now half hidden inside a grain sack.

Whump!

It knocked the breath out of both of them.

"You okay?" Holly gasped, rubbing her knee. She'd have a big old bruise in the morning.

From inside the sack, Twiggy's voice sounded muffled. Somehow, she'd gotten one arm stuck through a hole in the bottom and couldn't seem to pull it out. "Did I get him?"

"The coyote?"

"No, the big rabbit," Twiggy wailed. "Fluffet."

Fluffet?

Holly thought about all the barn cats they hadn't named as she untangled the princess from her musty old sack. Poor Twiggy. She was going to be heartbroken over this.

"Two got away," Holly said. "The little ones."

"But not Fluffet?"

Holly shook her head. Good thing Twiggy had been wrestling with the sack when it happened. That coywolf had snatched Fluffet by the scruff of his neck and taken off even faster than it had arrived. Was it the same animal she'd seen yesterday and again this morning?

Twiggy shivered. Luke ran up with a blanket and draped it around her shoulders. Pointing at the woods where the coywolf had been only moments before, she burst into tears. "Somebody, stop him."

"We can't," Luke said.

Twiggy cried even more. Her body shook so hard, Holly wrapped the sack around her as well. Maybe she was getting sick.

"Bring her inside," Kate called out. She'd just emerged from the barn's side door, with Angela behind her looking pale and scared. The horses were still neighing, but less frantically now. "It's warmer in here."

"No," Luke said. "I'll drive her home."

"What about Rebel?" Twiggy said as Luke helped her up. "It's too far for Kate to lead him back."

"I'll ride him," Holly said, plucking the helmet off Twiggy's head and cramming it onto her own. Good thing she'd worn her breeches and boots. Riding in shorts would've only added to her bruises.

"But you can't. Liz said—"

Holly almost choked. "When's the last time *you* obeyed orders?"

Twiggy gave a weak grin, then Luke said, "I could come back with my trailer and get the horses, if you like."

"Thanks," Holly said. "We'll be fine."

There was no sign of the coywolf, and the storm had finally let up. But, as she watched Luke leading Twiggy toward his truck, Holly almost wished she was going with them. The thought of riding back to Timber Ridge in a wet saddle on a wet horse with Angela complaining all the way made her cringe. On top of that, she and Kate were barely speaking to one another.

Maybe it was time to do something about that.

* * *

It was almost six when they got back to the barn. Mom was pacing her office looking halfway between frantic and furious, and Holly couldn't make up her mind if she was going to hug them or bawl them out.

In the end, she did both.

Luke had apparently filled her in before returning to Larchwood.

"Where's Charlotte?" Holly said.

Kate looked surprised. "She's here?"

"Luke brought her and Elke over this afternoon," Mom said. "She's gone home with Laura and Marcia, but she'll be here tomorrow."

"Okay, so where's Twiggy?" Holly said.

"Mrs. Dean came to get her," Mom said. "She's steaming mad, too."

"Why?"

"Because Kate took Angela and Twiggy on a dangerous trail ride."

"Oh, Mom," Holly said. "That's insane. You know it is. I bet it was Angela's idea, right, Kate?"

* * *

Right, Kate?

Just two little words—but they carried a big message. Kate exchanged a quick look with Holly, then followed her out of Liz's office and down the aisle. She knew, without a doubt, from Holly's grin that their silly feud was over—no need to spend hours analyzing each other's feelings or digging through emotions that Kate didn't understand. She'd never been any good at stuff like that, not the way Holly was.

"Yes," Kate said, looking around. There was no sign of Angela. Ragtime was in his stall; his wet saddle and bridle had been dumped on a tack trunk. "Twiggy cooked up this ride with Angela. I just tagged along."

"I *knew* it," Holly crowed.

Looking decidedly smug, she bounced into Magician's stall while Kate brushed Tapestry and fluffed up her bedding. Now that Holly's coyote sighting was no longer a myth—something else she'd be crowing to Kate about—they were keeping the horses inside until that rabid coywolf had been trapped.

"What'll they do to it?" Holly asked as they walked home across the back field. Liz was still in her office, juggling tomorrow's lesson schedule so she could fit in another team practice before Monday's tryouts.

"I don't know," Kate said. "But my father will."

Wearing a white butcher's apron, Dad was at the kitchen counter, expertly slicing onions. Ever since he and Liz had taken cooking lessons last winter, family meals had morphed from mac 'n' cheese in a box to fancy stuff like beouf bourguignon and chicken cordon blue.

Dad set down his knife. "They'll euthanize it, then—"

"Do they *have* to?" Holly wailed.

"No choice," Dad said, sounding sad. "A rabid animal is likely to bite another and spread infection. I'm afraid it's very dangerous, usually fatal." He looked at Holly. "Tell me what you saw. How close did that coywolf get to Twiggy? Did he touch her?"

"No," Holly said. "He was at least five feet away. He just grabbed the rabbit and took off."

"Are you sure?"

"Yes," Holly said. "Besides, Twiggy was stuck inside a grain sack."

Dad's bushy eyebrows shot up. "Why?"

"She was gonna use it to save the rabbits," Kate said.

"But her arm got caught," Holly continued, "and I had to pull her out. By then, the coywolf had snatched Fluffet, and—"

"*Fluffet?*" Kate said.

Holly rolled her eyes. "Yes."

"Then it sounds as if everything's okay," Dad said. "Well, except for that poor rabbit." He pinned them both with a look. "Just remember that coywolves and coyotes are part of nature, the circle of life, and—"

"Like in *The Lion King?*"

"Exactly."

Surprised, Kate looked at her father. She had no idea he'd even seen the film. His idea of a good movie was an obscure documentary about bugs in Borneo's rain forest that nobody outside of academia had ever heard of.

Holly began to hum a few bars.

"Coywolves have to eat," he went on. "Just like we do, and they only attack small animals, not humans."

"What if they're rabid?" Kate said.

Her father shook his head. "Even then, they're more afraid of you than you are of them. But let this be a lesson to all of you. Pay attention when you're in the woods. Don't interfere with the natural order of things like

Twiggy did. You can't save every squirrel, chipmunk, and bunny from being eaten. If you did, we'd be overrun with them."

"Poor Fluffet," Holly said.

Dad scooped onions into the frying pan. "You'd better get changed for dinner. You girls smell like a wet barn."

Giggling, Kate raced down the hall behind Holly. Their room didn't look as messy as it had this morning, or else she didn't care anymore. "Mrs. Dean's not gonna like this."

"No kidding," Holly said. She pulled off her breeches and dumped them on the floor. "And we'd better hope she keeps quiet about it, too. Twiggy won't want her father to know. He'd drag her home, for sure."

Yesterday, Kate would've thought this was a good thing, but now that she'd gotten to know Twiggy better, she didn't want her to leave. Besides, it was exciting having her around. The princess had been here just over a week, and already she'd been the catalyst for two hair-raising adventures.

"Oh, Mrs. Dean will keep quiet," Kate said.

"How do you know?"

"Bad publicity," Kate said, resisting the urge to pick up Holly's pile of wet clothes. "If word got out that Timber Ridge had a rabid coywolf running loose, Mrs. Dean wouldn't be able to sell any more houses."

12

Twiggy allowed herself a few more tears over poor old Fluffet, then pulled herself together. She'd been a complete and total idiot. After reaming her out for disobeying orders, Meredith had told her what would've happened if that coywolf had bitten her.

Tests, lots of tests. In a hospital.

Ugh, awful.

Dad would've dragged her back to England for sure. But driving home with Luke had been a blast. In the middle of telling her a corny joke that she'd heard a million times before, he'd asked about Kate, kind of casually, as if he didn't really care about the answer.

Did he like her?

More important, did Kate like him? Later, she'd ask Holly. But right now, they all had to get through another killer practice with Liz. Twiggy saddled Rebel and rode him into the outdoor ring. Kate, Holly, and Robin were already there, warming up. Angela was still in the barn fussing with Ragtime, and Kristina was trying to help her.

Six riders. Three spots on the team.

Twiggy knew she wouldn't make it, not on somebody else's horse, anyway. Besides, she wasn't good enough, and that was okay. One day she *would* be good enough. In the meantime, she'd quiz the others on horsemanship. She'd groom and clean tack, even for Angela, never mind that she didn't deserve to be on the team, either.

Last night over dinner—broccoli, again—Mrs. Dean had announced she'd invited lots of friends to come and watch Angela competing on Sunday, as if it were a foregone conclusion that she'd make the team. For a few seconds, Angela had turned deathly pale like she had that afternoon over the coywolves. Then she'd smiled and chattered on about how well Ragtime was going and that he'd be in top shape by the weekend.

Twiggy didn't envy Meredith.

She was caught between a rock and a hard place. Pick Angela and the team suffered. Bypass her and Mrs. Dean would complain. She'd probably spread ugly rumors about Meredith like she had when Meredith first arrived. None was true—Holly and Twiggy had managed to prove it—but Mrs. Dean didn't care.

If only Meredith wasn't leaving.

So far, her dad hadn't found another suitable body-guard, and Twiggy hoped he wouldn't—at least for an-other three weeks. By then she'd be flying home, and the first thing she would do was hug Diamond.

Did he miss her?

Probably not, now that he had Buccaneer for com-pany. Those two horses had become almost inseparable, like Tapestry and Magician were. Twiggy patted her empty pockets. She'd make sure to have plenty of water-melon rinds for Diamond and peppermint candy for Buc-caneer when she got to Beaumont Park.

The others finally arrived and after warming up, Liz had them all trotting in twenty-meter circles. No stirrups again. Twiggy wasn't sure she'd survive.

But she did.

Liz had set up an easy jump course alongside the higher one, just for Twiggy, which meant a lot of extra work lugging rails and uprights about and making sure the distances worked.

"Why?" Twiggy had asked Holly.

"Mom doesn't want you to feel left out."

"She's the best," Twiggy said, and managed to clear her special jumps without scattering rails.

Kate and Tapestry were brilliant over the higher jumps. So were Holly and Magician. Even Angela put in a good performance, which wasn't hard to do, given what a peach

Ragtime was. But Chantilly pulled up lame. Quickly, Liz examined her hoof and diagnosed a stone bruise.

Robin looked stricken. "Will she be okay?"

"Yes, but not in time for this weekend," Liz said. "Soak her foot in warm water and Epsom salts. There's a box in the tack room."

"Oh, bad luck," Angela said.

Kristina gave a smirky smile and Twiggy knew exactly what was going through her devious little mind.

Only five riders left.

* * *

If Monday had eyeballs, Kate would scratch them out. Not only was rain pounding the indoor's metal roof, but Mrs. Dean was now perched on a folding chair in the observation booth, making Kate more nervous than ever. So far, Angela's mother hadn't blasted her for Saturday's trail ride. She probably had some other punishment in mind.

"Duh-uh," Holly said. "This is it."

Miserably, Kate had to agree. Having Mrs. Dean at the tryouts made everyone uncomfortable, including Angela, who didn't look too thrilled that her beady-eyed mother was watching their every move. Not that she knew what they were doing—Mrs. Dean couldn't tell a canter from a cantaloupe.

Behind her sat Charlotte and Laura, with Marcia squashed between them. Kate was kind of surprised. Now that Mr. and Mrs. Dean were divorced, Marcia normally avoided her former stepmother like the plague. Charlotte giggled and gave Kate a thumbs-up.

Meredith called for an extended trot. Earlier, she'd given them a verbal quiz, followed by taking their bridles apart and putting them back together again. It wasn't a race, exactly, but Holly was the fastest, then Kate, and Twiggy a surprising third. She'd looked very pleased with herself. But Kristina had forgotten to attach Cody's browband, and Angela had buckled her reins to the bit inside out.

"This is stupid," she'd declared.

She'd done an even worse job of wrapping Ragtime's legs. He'd stood on the crossties, patient as ever, with white bandages unfurling around him like toilet paper. But right now, Angela was acing it, thanks to her brilliant horse. Nose tucked, Ragtime floated across the diagonal, feet barely seeming to touch the ground.

He scored over the jumps as well—one after the other in classic form. Would this cancel out Angela's miserable performance in horsemanship? Kate had no idea. Maybe riding counted for more than mucking stalls and cleaning tack. The show rules didn't say, or else Kate had missed them.

"Your turn, Kate," Meredith called out.

There were only five jumps—two oxers, a panel, parallel bars, and the dreaded coop. Instead of wings, the coop had wooden cutouts of huge chickens on each side—

painted brown, yellow, and bright orange—and Tapestry hated it.

Sitting deep in the saddle, Kate cantered a small circle, then lined up the first jump, a single red-and-white oxer. Over they went, then cleared the green parallel bars, followed by the rustic panel and a double oxer. Tapestry tipped the top rail, but it didn't fall.

Last up was the coop.

Kate softened her hands. If she didn't, her tension would flow down the reins into Tapestry's sensitive mouth. As she rode past the observation booth, she could almost feel Mrs. Dean's eyes boring into her like a dentist's drill. One of the little girls—Laura, maybe—squealed.

Tapestry hesitated. Kate used her legs, her voice, urging the mare forward with everything she had. They'd been through this many times before. Last year she'd bribed Tapestry over the coop with carrots, but that wouldn't work at a show. The judges wouldn't appreciate her tossing carrots over a jump for Tapestry to follow.

"C'mon," Kate said. "Let's go."

If she wasn't holding the reins, she would have crossed her fingers—her toes as well, except there wasn't room inside her boots. The coop threatened, looming closer and closer. Tapestry dodged left, then right. But Kate had anticipated that and pulled her horse back on track. Just one more stride, and—

No, too soon.

With an almighty lurch, Tapestry lifted off and soared over the coop like a gazelle. She'd obviously decided that if she couldn't run away from it, the only alternative was to jump it as big as possible.

Whump!

They landed so hard, Kate lost her stirrups.

* * *

The minute Twiggy marched into the tack room and closed the door behind her, Holly knew there was something on the princess's mind. It could be anything from her father's latest phone call to worrying about Meredith's replacement.

"What's up?" Holly said.

"Does Kate like him?"

"Who?"

Twiggy sighed as if Holly were a total idiot. "Luke Callahan."

"I dunno," Holly said.

She really didn't. She could only guess, because trying to figure out what Kate was feeling was harder than solving quadratic equations—not that Holly knew how to solve those, either.

"Oh, c'mon. You know she does."

"Okay, then, yeah, I guess." Holly dropped the bit she was cleaning. "But you know Kate. She's hopeless with guys."

When it came to boyfriends, Kate's track record was off-the-charts awful. She got tongue-tied or said the wrong thing . . . well, except for the night she'd slammed into Nathan Crane for being a jackass at the *Moonlight* premiere in New York.

He'd totally deserved it.

Then there was Brad Piretti, whose parents had run the Timber Ridge ski area ever since Holly could remember. Brad was a local snowboarding star, and he'd actually learned to ride because he liked Kate. Then he'd taught her to ski. But everything had gone toes up when Mrs. Dean fired Brad's father and nobody would talk about it, especially Brad and his sister Sue, who'd been on the riding team. The family had left town under a cloud of silence.

Twiggy said, "Luke asked me about Kate."

"Really?" Holly said.

"Yeah, driving home. He was kind of casual, like it was no big deal."

"But it was?"

"Yeah," Twiggy said. "I think so."

"Cool," Holly said. She'd wanted to get Luke and Kate together ever since he'd admired Tapestry at the end-of-camp horse show and told Angela to get lost when she'd called his sister's Norwegian Fjord an ugly cart horse. The only trouble was how to pull it off. "Got any ideas?"

"About what?"

"Getting Luke and Kate together."

"No problem," Twiggy said. "We use the *meet me in the alley* approach."

"Like a spy film?"

"Close enough," Twiggy said.

"Okay, so how does it work?" Holly wasn't too sure about this, but she was willing to try almost anything. Kate and Luke would be perfect together. They both loved horses, they had the same dreams, and neither one seemed to realize that the other was remotely interested.

Twiggy opened the door and peered both ways down the aisle like Nancy Drew on a mission. "Easy, peasy," she whispered. "At the horse show we tell Kate to meet us at the snack bar."

"Which one?"

"Doesn't matter," Twiggy said airily. "There'll be a ton of them. Doughnuts, coffee, pizza—whatever works."

"Okay, then what?"

"We get Adam to tell Luke the same thing."

Holly thought for a moment. "But we don't show up, right?"

"You got it," Twiggy said.

"Sounds kind of sneaky."

"Of course, it is," Twiggy said, grinning. "It's diabolically sneaky, and it'll work. Trust me."

But even as she agreed to go along with Twiggy's plan, Holly had her doubts. Kate would probably see through it because this was the way they'd maneuvered Mom and Kate's dad together by giving them both cooking lessons at the high school for Christmas.

Would Kate fall for it? Would Luke?

"Just one thing," Holly said. "If my sister has a meltdown over this, I'm gonna tell her it was *your* idea."

"Deal," Twiggy said.

* * *

Meredith's results appeared at nine the next morning on Liz's white board. In big letters, it said:

Angela Dean
Holly Chapman
Kate McGregor
Reserve: Kristina James

Kate slapped Holly on the back and heaved a huge sigh of relief. She'd really been sweating this one, convinced that Mrs. Dean would find a way to blackmail Meredith into keeping her off the team.

"Brilliant," Twiggy said, hugging first Holly and then Kate. "I'll be your flunky, okay?"

"Thanks," Kate said, "but it's not allowed."

"Seriously?" Twiggy frowned. "Meredith said she's going to help Liz."

"That's different," Holly said, as her mother walked through the door. "They're trainers, not competitors."

Twiggy's eyes widened. "You mean I can't even muck stalls or clean tack? Groom your horses?"

"I'm afraid not," Liz said, then ran through the rules. The teams' riders had to do everything for themselves, including answering questions on the fly from judges who'd be cruising the barns with clipboards and critical eyes.

"Okay, so I'll quiz you," Twiggy said, looking at Angela. "What's the difference between a Dartmoor and an Exmoor?"

"That's dumb," Angela retorted. "Those are English ponies, and they're not gonna ask questions like that."

"Okay, so what about a Danish Warmblood and an American Saddlebred?" Twiggy said. "They're very different, but how?"

Angela opened her mouth and shut it again. She looked at Kristina who shrugged.

Holly said, "You'd never use a Saddlebred for dressage."

"Why not?"

"It's a matter of the way horses are built," Kate said. "Some, like Thoroughbreds, are really good for jumping and cross-country; others are better suited for dressage or cutting cows."

Kristina rolled her eyes. "You wouldn't cut cows with a Saddlebred."

"True," Holly said. "You'd use a Quarter Horse."

"Or a Morgan," Kate added.

Liz intervened. "Just study up on your hoof ailments and stop arguing about breeds. They're all horses, and they're all pretty marvelous. We're lucky to have them."

"Even Przewalski's horse?" Holly said, grinning.

"Yes," her mother replied. "Especially that one, even though I can't pronounce it."

13

THE TIMBER RIDGE TEAM left for the Classic at dawn on Friday morning. Meredith sat up front beside Liz, clutching a large thermos of coffee that they passed back and forth. In the truck's back seat, Kate, Holly, and Twiggy watched *International Velvet* on Holly's iPod. Mrs. Dean had already driven off with Angela and Kristina, leaving their horses for everyone else to deal with.

Typical, Kate thought.

Whatever had prompted Angela to act almost normal a few days ago had now vanished. The old Angela was back in full force. Last night, she'd complained loudly about having to groom Ragtime and clean his tack.

"What's the point?" she'd grumbled, slopping way too much soap onto Ragtime's saddle and not rubbing it in properly. "It'll only get messy again."

"And so will you," Holly had gleefully pointed out. "You'll have an orange butt."

Traffic slowed as they approached the show grounds. Inching along behind a horse trailer with New Hampshire plates, it took them twenty minutes to cover half a mile.

"We'll be late," Holly said.

Her mother glanced in the rearview mirror. "Don't worry. We have plenty of time. You guys aren't riding till this afternoon."

Kate rolled down her window and peered outside. Against a backdrop of hazy mountains, she saw blue-and-white-striped tents with bunting and flower boxes, a covered grandstand overlooking a jumping ring, and low bleachers along both sides of a dressage arena. Flags fluttered; a loud, raspy voice tested the public address system.

"One, two, three."

A man wearing a Day-Glo yellow vest directed them to the field reserved for parking. Off to one side, Kate saw a cluster of long, metal buildings—the stables. People bustled about carrying buckets, brooms, and pitchforks. Two Jack Russell terriers raced in circles, yapping and getting in everyone's way.

Horses and riders warmed up in the practice ring. Trainers yelled instructions; parents stood at the rail, huddled in groups and sipping coffee. Two girls on warmbloods executed perfect half passes. Holly's boyfriend, riding his half-Arabian pinto, popped over a jump and narrowly missed colliding with a ramped-up Thoroughbred coming in the opposite direction.

"There's Adam," Holly squealed.

She ran toward him, arms outstretched and hair flying. It reminded Kate of a video that Holly loved.

Barefoot girl wearing layers of white gauze floats through a field of daisies. A boy runs toward her. His loose cotton shirt ripples in the breeze. They reach for one another, and . . .

Slow motion, soft focus, and hopelessly romantic. Except that Holly's torn jeans and faded t-shirt with "Boss Mare" on the back didn't quite fit the picture. Nor did her grubby paddock boots. With a goofy grin, Adam leaned down and hugged her. Their arms locked, and, for a heart-stopping moment, it looked as if he were about to fall off his horse.

Twiggy aimed her iPhone. "They should make a movie of this."

"Don't tell Holly," Kate warned, "or she'll want to."

Something hot surged up her throat.

Was she jealous? Of Holly and Adam? They'd been dating since last summer—the perfect teenage horse couple. They squabbled, noisily, and made up. Holly was famous for punching Adam; he always laughed her off. Riding for different teams, they'd competed head-to-head at horse shows and had cheered for one another, no matter if they'd won or lost.

Somehow, they made it work.

And watching them now, Kate wished she had someone special in her life who loved horses the way Adam did. Nathan Crane hadn't even come close, but Brad Piretti had tried his best. He'd even learned to post on Marmalade, and—

Kate swallowed hard.

She didn't have time to worry about her lack of a boyfriend right now. She was here to compete and help Timber Ridge do the best it could.

On the ride over, Liz had explained that there were no individual medals at this show. Just team ribbons and a challenge cup that had to be won three years in a row before a team could keep it forever.

Kate knew that Stonewall Farm, a big show barn in New Jersey, had already won it twice. Their trainer was rumored to be ruthless, that he'd pull out all the stops for a third win. His riders probably would, too.

Skillfully, Liz backed the Timber Ridge gooseneck into a parking spot, yelled at Holly to come and help, and told the others to unload their horses.

* * *

"What do you mean, no individual medals?" Angela glared at Kate, hands on both hips as if she were about to throw a tantrum. "They *always* have them."

"Not this time," Kate replied.

Angela's eyes narrowed. "How do you know?"

"Liz told us," Twiggy said. "In the van. There are team prizes and the challenge cup. Nothing else."

"That's stupid" Angela said, grabbing Kristina's hand. "C'mon, let's talk to my mother."

"Don't be an idiot," Holly said. "She can't do anything."

"Wanna bet?"

"Hey," Kate said. "What about Ragtime?"

She'd unloaded Angela's horse, removed his shipping bandages, and settled him into his stall. But he needed a thorough grooming. Bits of hay clung to Ragtime's tail, his mane was a snarly mess, and he'd managed to get manure stains on both hocks.

It was only a matter of time before the judges showed up. So far they hadn't come into C barn where Timber Ridge was stabled.

Diagonally across the aisle was Stonewall Farm. Their uniformed grooms had already bent the rules by setting everything up, while the four riders had hung about, drinking Evian water and complaining because the barn's air conditioners weren't cranked up high enough. Kate wondered if any of them even knew how to tighten a girth or adjust their stirrups.

Timber Ridge had five stalls—one for each of their horses and another for tack, feed, and equipment—but Stonewall Farm had seven.

Occupying four of their stalls were two highly polished light bays, a dappled gray, and a liver chestnut. They wore matching leather halters and had brass nameplates on their doors. The other three stalls, framed in black drapes with swags and gold tassels, served as a combination tack room and living room. Coach lanterns and fake trees flanked the entrance. Beyond it, Kate caught a glimpse of soft lighting, über expensive saddles and bridles, and two bored-looking girls slouched in overstuffed armchairs, texting madly—probably to each other.

Angela pointed. "That's what we need."

"Wrong," Kate snapped. "What we need is for you to take care of your horse."

"He's fine."

"Bratface," Holly muttered as Angela took off with Kristina.

Kate grabbed a brush. There was nothing in the rules that said riders couldn't help each other. But this wasn't about helping Angela. It was about team survival. Those judges would be along at any minute, and Ragtime hadn't even been braided yet.

* * *

Twiggy hated feeling useless. Her fingers itched to help. "What can I do?"

"Food," Holly said. "I'm starving."

"I'm on it," Twiggy said, leaping off Holly's tack trunk. This would give her a chance to scope out the snack bars so they could mastermind that "chance" meeting between Kate and Luke.

So far, there'd been no sign of him. Twiggy didn't even know which barn Weathervane Farm was in, but it wouldn't take much sleuthing to find out.

Holly had said that Luke wasn't competing. He was a show jumper not a three-day eventer, but he was here to help his father with the team, and he'd brought along a new horse just to give it the experience of being at a busy show. As Twiggy walked down the aisle, one of the Stonewall Farm girls stood up. A gold navel ring poked out from beneath her black crop top that had Stonewall's logo on the front.

"Are you with *that* team?" she said, nodding toward the Timber Ridge stalls.

The other girl yawned. "They're losers."

Twiggy ignored them. No matter what she said, even if it was the most brilliant comeback in the world, those girls wouldn't listen. They were like the girls at school—spoiled, rich, and selfish—and they'd probably never mucked a stall or cleaned tack in their lives. Be interesting to see how they managed without their grooms.

Before picking up snacks, Twiggy cruised the other two barns. She found Adam grooming Domino on the crossties in barn A. The Larchwood stalls were draped in red and black; Adam wore a matching t-shirt with his team's logo on the back. Red tack trunks with black lettering stood in front of each stall.

"Where are you guys stabled?" he said.

"C barn," Twiggy said, and pulled a face. "Across from Stonewall Farm."

"Watch out for them."

"Why?" Twiggy said. "They're just a bunch of snotty girls."

"They want to win."

"Hah," Twiggy replied. "So does Timber Ridge."

"Yeah, but—" Adam's voice trailed off as two judges strolled toward them, making notes as they looked in stalls and asked questions.

Twiggy stood back while they observed Adam brushing Domino and picking out his feet. One of the judges pointed at Domino's hock.

"What joint does that correlate to in a human?"

"The heel," Adam said.

"And this one?" The other judge bent down and gently touched Domino's right knee. His skin twitched, as if a fly had just landed.

Adam held up his hand. "The wrist."

After inspecting Domino's stall, both judges nodded, then continued down the aisle. Twiggy waited till they were out of earshot, quizzing another team. She rounded on Adam. "You're friends with Luke Callahan, right?"

Adam slapped his gelding on the rump and told him to move over. "Yup, we're best buddies."

"Do me a favor?"

"Okay, sure."

She had to get this right. Mess it up, and Adam would laugh. The best thing was to be totally honest. Not hide behind half-truths and beat about the bush the way girls would.

Guys didn't do that.

You had to hit them over the head. You had to be totally direct, or they wouldn't get it, especially when it came to feelings.

"Does he like Kate?"

Adam didn't even hesitate. "Yeah."

"But he's not sure that she likes him."

"You got it."

Great, now they were on the same track. Maybe guys weren't so different after all. But it had to be scary, wondering if a girl liked you and then taking a chance by asking her out, only to get shot down because she thought you were a creep.

It was kind of like those awful dances at middle school

that Holly had told her about, where the boys sat in a long line on one side of the gym and the girls sat on the other while the DJ went nuts trying to get everyone onto the dance floor. At least Twiggy hadn't had to deal with that.

Her school was girls only.

No boys allowed. She took a deep breath and checked the aisle again. This was going to be easy-peasy—just like she'd told Holly.

14

KATE'S MEMORY TURNED to rubble the moment she approached the dressage arena. The test that she'd so carefully rehearsed with Holly was nowhere to be found. She couldn't even remember whether to turn left or right after trotting down the centerline.

This had happened before.

Last summer, she'd been riding Magician in her first event for Timber Ridge when her mind had gone totally blank two seconds before she entered the ring. Holly had said not to worry because her horse knew the test. And he did.

But did Tapestry?

They'd practiced it often enough. As Kate halted and saluted the judge, she tried to clear her head, to think of something totally different, like guiding visitors around

Dad's butterfly museum or getting stranded on a black diamond ski trail last winter.

Now *that* had been scary.

From the corner of her eye, Kate saw Holly holding the test in her hand. If only she could peek over her sister's shoulder. Then, slowly, Holly turned toward the right as if she knew exactly what Kate was going through.

Perfect.

Just the clue Kate needed.

After that, it all came flooding back. She guided Tapestry through the familiar moves as if in a trance. The dressage markers floated past like alphabet soup.

> *Working trot from F to E. Ten-meter circle. Lengthen stride across the diagonal from M to K. Back to a working trot. Walk from F to C . . . at H, pick up a working canter—*

This wasn't very exciting. It didn't dazzle spectators like a Grand Prix performance set to music with piaffes and spectacular pirouettes. But it was hugely important—a building block.

Baby steps.

You couldn't train a horse for three-day eventing—or much of anything else—without the basics of dressage. They even had Western dressage these days. Some people said dressage was too highbrow, that ordinary horses didn't need it. But they obviously had no clue that *dressage* was just a word that meant "training" in French. And that's what you did with a horse.

You trained it.

In what felt like the blink of an eye, her test was over. Kate patted Tapestry, then left the ring on a loose rein as Angela trotted past.

"Good luck," Kate said.

No response. Angela's face was pale, her smile thin-lipped and tight. But Ragtime wasn't the least bit fazed. Despite his nervous rider, he put in a flawless performance.

"That's why he cost a bazillion dollars," Holly said.

"*Two* bazillion," Twiggy corrected. "Angela told me."

Thirty minutes later, Kate crossed her fingers as Holly and Magician took their turn in the dressage arena. Dropping his nose, the big black horse didn't put a foot wrong. He didn't even flub up his leads, and Kate knew that Holly had been sweating those.

Meredith slapped Holly's boot. "Good job."

"This should put us in the top five," Liz said, "as long as you guys didn't mess up on stable management."

"No way," Holly said.

She looked about to complain that Angela had flaked off, but she shut her mouth. Kate was glad. No matter what, the team had to stick together. Liz had enough on her mind without worrying about Angela's latest melt-down over the lack of individual medals.

Whatever she'd said to her mother hadn't done the trick. Scowling like a toddler, Angela had flounced back into the barn with the faithful Kristina trailing behind.

"How'd it work out?" Holly had said. "Did Mommy change the rules?"

"None of your business," Angela had snapped.

Then she'd grabbed a muck bucket and stomped into Ragtime's stall, but Kate had already cleaned it up. And just in time, too. Moments later, the judges had cruised past, making notes on their clipboards, and had moved across the aisle to check out the picture-perfect Stonewall Farm.

Nothing out of place, thanks to their invisible grooms.

* * *

The next day was cross-country. With their solid dressage scores, Timber Ridge had edged into fourth place—just a few points behind Larchwood and Weathervane. Stonewall Farm was in the lead.

No big surprise.

Holly was the last Timber Ridge rider to go. At two thirty she blasted out of the starting gate with Magician. Five minutes behind them came Adam and Domino. As she cleared the first fence, Holly wondered if her boyfriend would try to catch up.

This wasn't a race.

You didn't win points by going faster than anyone else.

You got penalties for refusals and missed fences, along with time faults for being too slow. Kate had already ridden the course and said it wasn't nearly as tough as it had looked when they'd walked it earlier that morning. Angela had one refusal.

"Watch out for the crowd," she'd warned.

"Where?"

"The Trakehner."

It wasn't a big jump—two heavy rails over a ditch— and it came up next. Ropes lined the approach with a scatter of spectators behind them. Officials in blue windbreakers tried to keep kids and dogs from straying onto the course.

Magician flicked his ears. He wanted to rush the fence, but Holly held him back. *One, two*, she counted, and was about to add *three* when it happened . . . *in the blink of an eye*.

A tiny dog, no bigger than a cat, catapulted out of someone's arms, and Magician slammed on the brakes. If he hadn't, they'd have run the dog over.

Heart thumping like sneakers in a dryer, Holly pulled her scattered wits together. If she turned away, backed up, or circled, it would count as a refusal, but if she kept Magician pointing at the jump and they managed to get over it from a standstill, she wouldn't get any faults.

The Trakehner was pretty low. Magician could probably step over it. Shifting into a two-point position, Holly decided to risk it. The worse that could happen was that Magician would balk and they'd be penalized. Blasting the officials about the dog would get her nowhere.

Instead, she tightened her grip and kicked Magician forward. She hadn't worn spurs because he never needed them, not even now.

"C'mon, guy," she whispered.

Her wonderful horse didn't let her down. Magician lifted himself up and catapulted over the jump, landing well clear of the ditch. Cheers erupted.

A voice yelled, "Well done."

Holly cantered on. This had cost them a few seconds. She'd have to speed up a bit. There were apps you could download to your iPhone that measured the distance between cross-country jumps, recommended the best angles, and told you how fast to go. The Vermont Classic's rules banned these apps, but Holly was willing to bet that Stonewall Farm used them.

* * *

As Twiggy waited for Holly to finish the cross-country, she saw one of the Stonewall Farm riders warming up near the start gate. It was the girl with the navel ring, and she was getting yelled at by her weasel-faced trainer. Another man hovered nearby, a rag hanging from his back pocket. A groom, probably. Twiggy stared at him.

He stared back, looking shifty-eyed.

It was the same man Twiggy had seen yesterday, hauling a muck bucket out to the manure pile after the judges had come by. He'd looked over his shoulder, constantly, as if expecting to be slammed at any minute. The Stonewall Farm girls had acted like he wasn't even there.

To them, he wasn't.

He was just another nameless person in a long line of workers who mucked stalls, groomed horses, and cleaned tack for rich girls who'd never been required to do it for themselves. Twiggy gave an exasperated sigh.

Her parents were rich. Superrich. They could buy this entire horse show and all its competitors, their horses, and their fancy stud farms six times over, but that wasn't how you coped with your wealth—at least, not where Twiggy came from. But this was a different world.

Money talked.

But so did brains. Twiggy gave hers a good shake. She sorted everything out and decided that Stonewall Farm wasn't to be trusted.

Best to keep an eye on them.

Just the way Kate's father had told them to keep an eye on the coywolves. *Be alert, but don't interfere unless you have to.*

* * *

Holly got back with ten seconds to spare. She'd gone clear over the course, and so had Adam, galloping up just a few minutes behind her. But one of the Stonewall Farm girls had racked up three time faults and was now getting yelled at by her furious trainer.

"Poor thing," Holly said, flinching.

"Don't feel sorry for *her*," Twiggy said. "She is *so* basic."

After cooling Magician off, Holly settled him back in his stall, fluffed up his bedding, and made sure his fly sheet was buckled correctly. She'd heard a rumor that someone on the Spruce Hill team had been slammed for having a twisted strap.

"They're back," Twiggy whispered.

"Who?"

"The judges."

Holly closed Magician's door. Was her hair a mess? Did she have mud on her boots, her breeches? Well, too bad. She'd just ridden a cross-country course and had taken care of her horse before taking care of herself.

The woman judge asked Holly to identify five snaffles. She rattled them off—eggbutt, D-ring, Mullen-mouth, jointed, full cheek—and didn't even hesitate when the guy judge asked her to name the first Triple Crown winner. They'd had this question at The Festival of Horses and Angela had been the only one to get it right. For some peculiar reason it had stuck inside Holly's head like an earworm.

"Sir Barton," she said.

Oh, no, wait a minute.

Maybe it was Sir Barclay. No, definitely Barton. But, whatever. Too late now to change it. Infuriatingly, the judge didn't react. He just made notes, then rubbed Magician's nose.

"Is this one yours?" he said.

"Yes."

Would he find something wrong? Was Magician's water topped up? Did he have enough hay? How many fragments of manure had Holly failed to pluck out of his bedding?

She bit back a sigh.

This was getting ridiculous. Horses drank water, they pooped in their stalls, and you couldn't keep it perfect twenty-four/seven.

"Nice horse," the woman judge said, then headed across the aisle to Stonewall Farm with the other judge trailing behind her.

Holly heaved a sigh of relief. Now, where was Kate? It was time to put the Kate-and-Luke plan into action.

"C'mon," she said to Twiggy. "Let's find Adam."

* * *

Horses trotted past as Kate stared at Holly's latest text.

"Coming through," someone yelled.

Automatically, Kate moved over. Mud splashed on her

boots. More globs landed on her face. She flicked them off, then wiped both messy hands on her breeches.

Oh, great.

Good thing the judges weren't cruising about. It was almost four thirty. The last cross-country scores had been posted. Timber Ridge was now in second place, a few points behind Stonewall Farm.

Let's celebrate, Holly's message said.

Kate typed, *Where?*

Coffee Shack. Right now!

Okay.

Kate wasn't in the mood for coffee, but maybe she'd have fruit juice or a pastry that would keep her going until dinner. Dodging around a trio of determined ponies, she headed toward the coffee stand. On one side was a mobile tack shop; on the other, an ice-cream cart with a red-and-white umbrella was doing a brisk business.

Plenty of people milled about, but nobody she recognized. Okay, so where was Holly? Her message had sounded urgent, like she absolutely *had* to have a coffee right away or she'd wither up and die.

The Coffee Shack's line snaked around the corner and out of sight. No point in standing in that. Ditto the ice-cream line.

Kate slumped onto a picnic bench. Riders, deep in conversation with their trainers, wandered past. Two girls wearing bright-yellow Spruce Hill shirts and clutching overloaded ice-cream cones asked if they could share Katc's table.

"Sure," Kate said, looking around.

Still no sign of Holly. If she didn't show up, like right now, Kate was going back to the barn. She'd celebrate with the horses instead. She gave her sister another minute and was about to fire off a snarky text when someone tapped on her shoulder.

"Kate, have you seen Adam?"

15

CROUCHED BETWEEN TWO trash barrels, Holly crossed her fingers and watched Luke Callahan touch Kate's shoulder. For a split second, Kate appeared to freeze, then she turned around and did what she always did whenever a guy was involved. She blushed. Even from this distance, Holly could tell it was a humdinger.

Poor Kate. If they ever invented an off switch for blushes, she'd be first in line to buy it. And Holly would be right there, making sure her sister got the best deal.

"Is it working?" Twiggy said.

Holly shoved the princess behind her. "Keep out of sight."

"I can't see."

"He's sitting down next to her. Oh, now they're talking."

"What are they saying?"

Holly tried to read Kate's lips, to see the expression on her face, but Luke kept getting in the way. Then they both scanned the crowd as if expecting to see Adam and Holly appear at any minute. Luke shook his head; Kate shrugged and stood up.

"No," Twiggy wailed, leaning over Holly's shoulder. "She can't leave."

"Sshh," Holly warned. "They'll hear you."

*　*　*

The rational, sensible half of Kate wanted to stay. The other half that was now blushing redder than a second-place ribbon wanted to leave—as fast as possible. This was obviously a setup, and when she got her hands on Holly, she would strangle her.

Luke said, "Don't leave."

"I gotta go."

"Why?"

Because I'm going to kill my sister.

He really did have the most amazing eyes. Green? No, blueish green. They crinkled at the corners, especially when he smiled—which he was doing now. Kate's blush deepened. Pretty soon she'd self-combust.

She had to get away.

But she couldn't because Luke had taken her hand and was pulling her back onto the bench, *next to him*. Across the table, the ice-cream girls were nudging each other and whispering. One of them thrust a crumpled show program toward Luke.

"Could you, um, sign it?" she squealed.

The other one giggled. "Mine, too."

"Yeah, sure," Luke said. "Got a pen?"

Now Kate really wanted to escape. She'd been through this with Nathan Crane—groupies, fans, and autograph hunters. While Luke was rummaging in his pockets for something to write with, Kate slipped away. He wouldn't even notice, and that was fine.

No, it wasn't.

Why did this always happen to her? Why couldn't she fall for an ordinary guy like Adam Randolph? Brad Piretti didn't count. He wasn't exactly ordinary, given half the town of Winfield had worshipped him for being a snow-boarding star and the other half had followed his every move on the high school's football field.

A hot tear rolled down Kate's cheek.

Angrily, she wiped it off. This was ridiculous. She'd had all of two, maybe three, conversations with Luke Callahan, and now she was mad because—

Why?

Her foot caught a rut. Backing up, she kicked it hard enough to hurt her toes. "Ouch."

"Feel better?"

Kate whirled around and would've fallen if he hadn't

caught her arm. "Go away," she said, feeling decidedly wobbly. "Your fans are waiting."

"They could be yours, too," Luke said.

"What does that mean?"

"It means you're good enough to go far."

"How do you know?"

"Because I watched your dressage test and your cross-country ride," he said, still holding her arm. Kate yanked herself free, then wished she hadn't. His fingers had felt good, as if they belonged.

How stupid was this?

"Where?" Kate said. She hadn't noticed him on the course. Then again, there'd been a ton of spectators out there. And dogs . . . lots of dogs.

Luke pulled an iPhone from the side pocket of his cargo pants. He wiped the screen with the hem of his t-shirt and handed it to her. "Here you are."

In a daze, Kate saw herself jumping the palisade, splashing through the water hazard, and scrambling over the coffin. Tapestry hated that jump almost as much as she hated chicken coops, but she hadn't balked.

"Oh," Kate said. "Thank you."

Luke tucked the phone back into his pocket. "You have a ton of talent and your mare is amazing, but—"

"What?" Kate said, even though she knew exactly what was coming. She'd heard it all before, from Liz and Meredith and from several trainers who'd given clinics at

Timber Ridge. Even Lockie Malone had said the same thing.

"—you need another horse."

"Yes, I know," Kate said, hating the truth. She stopped at the door to C barn. From inside, she could hear Magician and Tapestry whinnying at each another. "But right now I need to go and hug my unsuitable horse."

"Please," Luke said. "Don't be mad."

"I'm not."

"You are," he said. "You're furious, and I know exactly how you feel."

"Yeah, right," Kate retorted. "You've got the best horses in the world, and—"

"—I still love my first one the best," he said, surprising her. "She's living the life of luxury at my grandmother's farm. You must come and meet her."

"Your grandmother?"

"No, my horse," he said, laughing. "Well, both of them, actually." His blue-green eyes turned wistful. "Your Morgan's a dead ringer for my Cupcake."

Cupcake?

In a flood of mixed emotions, Kate's anger dissolved and drained away, right through the toes she'd just stubbed. "Okay," she said. "But I really must—"

"Heads up!" someone yelled.

Nostrils flaring, Ragtime erupted from the barn and took off at an extended trot as if he were performing a

Grand Prix dressage test. Seconds later, Angela emerged, red-faced and furious. Fists clenched, she rounded on Kate.

"You let him out," she screeched. "On purpose."

* * *

It took less than five minutes to capture the runaway horse. The moment Ragtime found grass, he'd stopped to eat and by the time Kate caught up to him, Angela's gelding was happily frisking Holly and Twiggy for treats.

"What happened?" Holly said, feeding him a carrot.

"He got out."

"How?"

"Angela seems to think I did it."

"But that's crazy," Twiggy said. "You were with Luke."

Holly punched her. "Shut up."

"Ouch," Twiggy said, rubbing her arm.

Kate let it go. They had bigger problems to worry about than Holly's latest matchmaking scheme. Like who conveniently forgot to latch Ragtime's stall? Not Angela, surely. Even she wouldn't be stupid enough to let her own horse out just so she could blame Kate for it.

"It was a careless mistake," Liz said, once Ragtime was safely back inside. "Angela, make sure his door is properly fastened from now on."

"But I did."

"Not this time," Liz said. "And check his legs for heat."

Angela struck a pose. "That's *your* job."

"No, it's yours."

Firmly, Liz took Angela's arm and led her into the Timber Ridge tack room. The door clicked shut, and Kate heaved a sigh of relief. It would've been awful if Liz had given Angela an earful in front of Luke Callahan.

He said, "Let's go."

"Where?"

"To see Tapestry."

Kate felt kind of shy about it, but Luke insisted he wanted to help Kate hug her horse.

"If she'll let me," he added. "Mares can be picky."

"Mine isn't."

He laughed. "Is that a compliment?"

Kate blushed, then slid open Tapestry's door. "Oh, no."

"What's wrong?"

Stunned into silence, Kate just stared, unable to believe her eyes. She'd been gone twenty minutes—half an hour, tops—and yet Tapestry's stall looked as if it hadn't been mucked out since yesterday morning. No, it was worse than that.

Much worse.

The fresh bedding she'd put down less than an hour ago was now littered with old manure. In the far corner, filthy bandages and snarls of baling twine spilled from a torn feed sack. Tapestry's water bucket had sprung a leak; her hay net hung empty and forlorn.

Kate had a horrible sense of déjà vu.

This was exactly what Angela had done to Magician's stall when she'd tried to sabotage Kate's chances for the individual medal at the Hampshire Classic last summer. But it wasn't Angela this time. Kate was sure of it.

From across the aisle, she heard muffled laughter.

Stonewall Farm?

"Looks like a war zone," Luke said, handing Kate a pitchfork. "Can I help?"

"Thanks, but you're not allowed."

Twiggy stuck her head over Tapestry's door. "Magician's stall is a mess, too."

"What about Ragtime's?"

"It's fine," Twiggy said. "But you'd better be quick. The judges are coming." She gave Luke a shove. "Keep them busy as long as you can."

He saluted. "Yes, ma'am."

* * *

Twiggy wanted to keep watch. She didn't trust those Stonewall Farm girls any farther than she could throw them. Everyone—including Luke and Adam—suspected they were behind Ragtime's escape and the messy stalls, but nobody could prove it.

"I'll sleep in the tack room," Twiggy offered.

As if that would do any good. She'd be out for the count most of the time. Her father always said she slept more deeply than anyone he'd ever known.

"Shifts," Kate said. "We could take turns."

But Angela didn't want to give up her plushy hotel bedroom. Neither did Kristina, which would've left three of them trying to cover too many hours with not enough sleep.

It didn't help, either, that the show committee had just announced that all the teams would be on parade at nine o'clock the next morning. A goodwill gesture, or something.

"More like PR," Holly grumbled.

After barn chores, Luke and Kate wandered off. At least that had worked out pretty well—for now, anyway. Twiggy hung about with Holly and Adam, drifting from one taco stand to another until Twiggy was ready to declare war on Mexico.

"My mouth's on fire," she complained.

Holly gave her a soda. "Wimp."

* * *

For once, Twiggy slept badly. Thanks to heartburn and worrying about sabotage, she woke up feeling as if she'd been fighting with her bed rather than sleeping in it.

Breakfast wasn't much better.

Yawning her way through cold scrambled eggs and even colder toast, Twiggy staggered into the barn ten minutes later to discover that their horses' hooves were now shocking pink.

"With glitter," Holly said.

Open-mouthed, they all stared. Every Timber Ridge horse, including Cody, sported hooves the color of Barbie's latest lipstick.

"Get the hoof polish," Kate said.

But there was none to be found. The cans in their tack stall were now empty, never mind they'd been mostly full the day before. Kate pulled out a dry brush and flung it on the ground. It landed at Luke's feet.

"Problems?" he said.

Twiggy shot him a grateful smile. In all the fuss, she hadn't even realized he'd shown up. Somehow, he'd slipped into the barn, unseen, and now stood beside Kate. Their hands were close enough to touch.

"We need help," Holly said. "Hoof polish."

"Why?" he said.

"This." Twiggy pointed at Magician, hooves sparkling, standing on the crossties like a fantasy horse from *Moonlight*. He looked kind of cute, but the judges would have a fit.

Glittery pink feet on a show jumper?

No way.

"Leave it to me," Luke said. "Don't do anything until I get back."

Taking Twiggy's hand, he pulled her out of the barn and straight toward the mobile tack shop. But instead of regular hoof polish, Luke bought six bottles of something bright pink called Sparkle and Shine.

"Why?" Twiggy said, confused.

It made no sense. If Luke wanted to help Timber Ridge, this wasn't the way to do it. They needed plain old black or brown hoof polish. The sticky kind, in a can, that you slopped on with a brush and were hugely grateful when you didn't spill it on the ground or get it all over your hands.

"Fight fire with fire," Luke said, grinning. "And trust me. I know what I'm doing."

Twiggy opened her mouth to argue, then shut it again. She didn't have a leg to stand on, but Luke did. He knew the American show circuit and all its peculiarities far better than she did.

16

KATE WAITED TILL THE LAST MINUTE. Liz had driven off at dawn to meet Dad for breakfast, so she wasn't around to make decisions. Except for Meredith, the girls were on their own.

The parade was about to begin, and the Timber Ridge horses had shocking pink feet. This would've been fine for a rodeo or the Tournament of Roses parade in Pasadena, but a three-day event in Vermont?

No way.

The show's loudspeaker hummed into life.

All teams, please assemble in the warm-up ring.

The Stonewall Farm girls sniggered as they rode past on their spotless horses with perfectly ordinary hooves. "Good luck, losers."

"Get lost," Kate snarled.

Angela led Ragtime from his stall and was about to mount when Holly said, "He's bobbing."

"What?" Angela said.

Her foot was already in the stirrup. Kate handed Tapestry's reins to Twiggy. She ran her hands down Ragtime's left foreleg and onto his hoof.

Warm.

Not a good sign.

"It's probably the glitter," Angela said.

Sadly, Kate shook her head. "No, he's lame."

Meredith confirmed Kate's diagnosis. "He must've injured himself yesterday—when he got loose."

"Okay," Holly said. "Now what do we do?"

"Two options," Meredith said. "Angela can ride Cody in the show jumping or Kristina can." She checked her watch, then looked at both girls. "It's your call. Figure out what you're comfortable with. You have two minutes to make a decision, and then I'll have to let the judges know."

* * *

Twiggy couldn't help grinning as one team after another fell into Luke's pocket when he handed out glitter and explained the problem.

"Sign us up," said the Spruce Hill coach.

"Oh, what fun," said the riders from Fox Meadow. "We *adore* pink glitter."

So did everyone else. They'd all been burned by Stonewall Farm at previous shows. One of the Larchwood girls gripped her bottle so hard, the lid flew off and splattered Luke's face with glitter.

"Oops, sorry," she said.

He laughed and raised a fist. "Pink power."

Adam thumped him on the back, then painted two generous coats of glitter onto Domino's feet.

"Go," Luke said to Twiggy. "And hurry."

At full speed, she raced past the Coffee Shack, the ice-cream stand, and the Stonewall Farm girls looking beyond smug as they rode toward the warm-up ring.

Boy, were *they* in for a shock.

"Where've you been?" Kate demanded. "And where's our hoof polish?"

"Don't need it," Twiggy said, breathing hard.

Kate pointed at Tapestry's feet. "We can't go out there like this."

"Yes, you can."

"Why?"

"Because *every*one else is," Twiggy said and told them how Luke had pulled the other teams into his brilliant plan. The entire show, with one notable exception, would be sporting bright pink hooves at the parade.

"Seriously?" Holly said.

Twiggy grinned. "Yes, seriously."

"The judges won't like it," Kate said.

Angela patted Cody's neck. "Too bad."

* * *

Despite Kate's misgivings, everyone cheered as the teams rode past the grandstand with all of their horses—except for Stonewall Farm—sporting glittery pink hooves. Even the stern-faced judges smiled, and the ring steward positively beamed.

"Way to go," he said.

Amid whoops and whistles, the teams made three more circuits and left the arena as Liz and Ben arrived with three excited little girls in tow.

"Classy," Liz said after Meredith explained how Luke had solved the hoof polish fiasco. "Did you call the vet for Ragtime?"

"Yup," Meredith said. "And it's minor. He should be fine in a week or so."

"Thanks." Liz put a hand on Luke's arm. "And thanks to you, too. I owe you one."

"It was fun," Luke said. With a smile, he pulled two bottles of glitter from his back pocket, bowed low, and presented one each to Marcia and Laura.

"For us?" Marcia squealed.

Laura grabbed Marcia and pretended to swoon, and as they danced about, Kate wondered if she'd have behaved the same way at their age.

Ten? Eleven?

She couldn't imagine it. Just one goofy grin from Luke, and the girls erupted in a peal of giggles. They ooh'd and aah'd and went all wobbly-kneed, just like a couple of kittens with catnip.

Well, wait a minute.

He had the same effect on her, especially with those blobs of pink glitter on his cheeks. For a mad moment, Kate wanted to reach out and touch them. Then she caught Holly's eye and gripped her reins instead.

Charlotte gave a theatrical sigh. "No big deal," she said in a stage whisper. "He's my idiot brother, and he's like this *all* the time."

* * *

The show jumping course wasn't difficult, just really colorful. Its designers had used every shade in a box of crayons, and then some.

"Purple?" Holly exclaimed.

Twiggy tossed her head. "*Royal* purple."

"No, *killer* purple," Angela said. Eyes flashing, she glared at the Stonewall riders, now warming up in the practice ring. "We'll bury them."

"You bet," Kate said.

It was an eye-opener, seeing Angela like this. Instead of gunning for Kate, she was now aiming her venom at Stonewall Farm. For once, Timber Ridge felt like a team.

A *real* team.

The positions had shifted a little, and Timber Ridge was now in third place. Stonewall Farm was still in the lead, but how long would that last once the judges found out they'd been cheating? *If* they found out. Would anybody rat on them?

"We can't," Kate said. "We have no proof."

Back to square one. Then Twiggy noticed that Stonewall had swapped a horse—one of their two look-alike bays. Was it more cheating? After Angela and Kristina had agreed that Angela should ride Cody, Meredith had gotten a judge to confirm that Ragtime was definitely lame. Swapping out horses and riders wasn't just something a team could do on a whim. There had to be a valid reason.

"Pay no attention," Liz said. "Ride the way you always do, and be glad that you've done your best." She hugged each of her riders in turn. "That's all I can ask."

Holly jumped a clear round. Angela and Cody had one rail down. Mrs. Dean looked about ready to tear Angela apart when Liz intervened and pointed out that jumping a horse you hadn't practiced on was a big challenge and that Angela had done a good job.

"If you say so," said Mrs. Dean.

Kate shot a look at Angela. "Well done."

"Thanks," Angela mumbled.

"What's the score?" said her demanding mother. "Are we in the lead yet?"

Patiently, Liz explained that nobody knew the variables about stable management and horsemanship and how they would affect the final results. "It's a moving target," Liz said. "We'll just have to wait. Now, Kate, are you ready?"

"Yes, I think so."

It pretty much rested on her shoulders. Go clear, and Timber Ridge would stay in the top ribbons. If not, then—

"You can do it," Luke said, slapping Kate a high five. His father's team had jumped clear and moved into second place. Stonewall was still in the lead.

Twiggy grinned. "Pressure, much?"

"Yeah," Angela said. "And good luck."

* * *

A little off balance, Kate cantered through the start gate without quite knowing how she got there. Angela's unexpected kindness had obviously unnerved her. She tightened her grip.

Concentrate, just concentrate.

First up was a yellow-and-white vertical flanked by window boxes. Kate cleared it easily, then hung a gentle left and popped over the gate. A brush jump came next—

Tapestry's front legs took out several twigs—followed by a hard right turn toward the in-and-out.

A blue-and-white ascending oxer came first, then a set of green parallel bars with two long strides between, or three short ones if your horse was small.

A tricky combination.

So far, this jump had produced two refusals and five knockdowns. Kate counted strides. She felt Tapestry hesitate.

"Go, girl," she said.

But Tapestry had other ideas. Her momentum was off. So was Kate's. At the last minute, Tapestry skidded to a halt.

Four faults.

The bottom rail wobbled in its cups, then crashed to the ground, narrowly missing Tapestry's legs. After the jump crew put the rail back up, Kate circled and tried again. Another refusal—or a knockdown—would probably put them out of the running.

"One, two, three, and . . ." Kate whispered.

This time, Tapestry didn't even hesitate. They cleared both parts of the combo, hung a sharp right turn, and leaped over the water jump. Jump six was the hogsback— three black-and-white rails with the center one higher than the other two. Beneath it was a bale of hay—a perfect snack for hungry horses.

"Don't stop," Kate warned.

Tapestry flicked her ears, then tucked her front legs and took off. Up and over the hogsback they went with room to spare. Two more jumps and they'd be done.

Carefully, Kate steered Tapestry in a shallow arc toward fence number seven. It was narrow and shockingly purple. On both sides were orange-and-purple wings shaped like a butterfly. Her father was probably loving it. At least it wasn't a chicken coop.

"C'mon," she urged.

Tapestry dodged right, then left, but Kate drove her forward with everything she had, and they soared over the butterfly fence at an awkward angle.

Clang!

Her left stirrup had caught an upright. Kate held her breath, waiting for it to fall. It didn't.

Phew.

One more to go. Even from this far off, the red wall looked very solid and very real, but Kate knew it was an illusion. Those bricks were lightweight. Earlier, Adam had gotten four faults by taking out the top row.

Kate steered Tapestry into an easy left turn. There was plenty of run-up and plenty of time to dredge up old memories. The first time she'd jumped a wall like this for Timber Ridge, she'd done it without stirrups on Holly's horse. But now she was on her own horse, and she still had both feet firmly in her stirrups.

A much better situation.

Most riders—and most horses—hated solid jumps because they couldn't see the other side. Even though this wall was pretty low—a shade above three feet—it was still intimidating, and it was getting closer.

Leaning forward, Kate placed her hands on either side of Tapestry's neck. Her old riding instructor used to say, "Throw your heart over a fence and follow it."

No problem.

Kate's heart was about to pop out of her mouth, anyway. Up and up went Tapestry. But not quite far enough. Her hind leg tipped a single brick and down it went.

No, no.

The crowd moaned. The finish gate flew by, and Kate heard the loudspeaker announce that she had eight faults. Just enough to keep them out of the top three.

"Don't worry about it," Liz said, as she threw a cooler over Tapestry's back. "You guys did fine out there."

"I flubbed up."

"It's not the end of the world, okay?"

"Thanks," Kate said, grateful that Liz wasn't yelling at her like other instructors would.

But it didn't help. All she wanted was to get away on her own for a bit. Holly rode up. She hesitated, then reached out and touched Kate's knee.

"Bad luck."

"No, bad riding," Kate muttered.

She'd let the team down, and she'd let her horse down. Even worse, Luke had seen her do it. He'd probably taken a video, too. Inwardly, Kate cringed. He wouldn't be so impressed with her now.

Not after this.

17

TWIGGY FELT AWFUL FOR KATE. She'd ridden off by herself, and even Holly hadn't gone with her. Everyone else was still milling around the warm-up ring, waiting for results.

Restless, Twiggy wandered back into the barn. The place was deserted. No sign of anyone, not even the Stonewall grooms. Their tack room loomed empty. She looked both ways.

All clear.

Darting inside, Twiggy scanned the room. Now that judging was over, the Stonewall crowd had left crumpled soda cans, plastic bags, and empty coffee cups lying about. A tack trunk yawned open, spilling dirty leg wraps and a balled-up black t-shirt with random patches of pink. Curious, Twiggy bent down for a closer look.

Footsteps sounded outside.

In a panic, Twiggy snatched up an empty plastic bag and stuffed the t-shirt inside.

Just in time, too.

The shifty-eyed groom said, "What you doin' here?"

"Nothing," Twiggy said, airily.

He glared at her. "Go away."

"Right," Twiggy said, and edged carefully toward the door, keeping the bag hidden behind her. The minute her feet hit the aisle, she was off—running as hard as she could for the show secretary's tent. That's where the judges were gathered, sorting out the final results.

A few yards away, she slowed down and took a deep breath. She had to handle this properly, the way her father would. People always listened to him. But, just to be absolutely sure she wasn't barking up the wrong tree, Twiggy checked her evidence again.

Perfect.

Those glittery pink smudges all over navel girl's black crop top were a dead giveaway. So was the team's logo.

Okay, what else would convince the officials that she wasn't totally insane? How about those ridiculous business cards her father had insisted on that Twiggy thought were useless?

Did she have any?

A frantic rummage in her wallet produced a single card—creased at one corner and not terribly clean. But its gold script was quite clear:

Princess Isabel of Lunaberg

Head up and shoulders back, Twiggy put on her royal face and stepped inside the tent. Whatever happened next, she would keep secret.

* * *

Even though Tapestry had cooled down, Kate kept on walking . . . and walking . . . and trying to think. Both Liz and Holly had told her not to beat herself up over this.

But she couldn't help it.

Those eight faults were *her* fault. Not Tapestry's. Not anybody's but her own.

Suddenly, the loudspeaker crackled into life. The final results would be delayed. "Just give us another twenty minutes, folks," said the announcer. "We appreciate your patience."

At this point, Kate didn't even care. Thanks to her, Timber Ridge wasn't going to place. Nobody had expected them to win, but getting third, or even fourth, would've been great. She'd have settled for fifth. Head down, she plodded on. Someone rode up beside her.

"You wanna talk about it?" Luke said.

Kate stiffened. "No."

"Think of it as a learning experience," he said. "It's what I always do."

"Like, when's the last time you messed up?" she said,

giving him a sideways glance. Luke was riding a stunningly gorgeous rose gray. This had to be his new horse, the one he was bringing along.

"Last week."

"Where?"

"HITS in Saugerties," Luke said, looking chagrined. "I had two refusals at the first fence and got eliminated."

Kate found it hard to swallow. He was so good, how on earth could this happen? "I don't believe you," she said. "You're just saying that to make me feel better."

Luke whipped out his iPhone. "Want me to prove it?"

"Don't bother."

"Look," he said, riding so close that his knee almost touched hers. "I know you'll be mad, but I took a video of your round. It might help if you watched it. I've been watching mine. Dad forces me to, like every day."

By now, they were at the barn door. Kate slid off Tapestry. She felt her mare's shoulder and between her front legs to make sure Tapestry really was cooled off.

Marcia held up Tapestry's halter. "Shall I take her?"

"Yes, please," Kate said. "And thanks."

Leading Tapestry, Marcia headed into the barn, with Laura and Charlotte skipping behind.

Luke said, "Great kids, even my bratty sister."

"She's not a brat."

"You don't have to live with her." He gave Kate a shy smile, then said, "I could use your help."

"When?"

"Tomorrow night," Luke said, playing with his horse's mane. "Are you busy?"

Was he asking her on a date? Kate felt herself blush and turned away. Then, out of nowhere, Holly, Adam, and Twiggy materialized. Had they been spying on her again? She still hadn't blasted Holly for setting her up yesterday.

Holly dug Kate in the ribs. "Go on, answer."

"Ladies and gentlemen," the loudspeaker interrupted. "Thanks for your patience. Here are the results of this year's Vermont Summer Classic. In first place—"

Kate's hands flew up to cover her ears, but Twiggy pulled them down. "Listen," she said. It sounded like an order.

"—we have Weathervane Farm. In second place, Larchwood, and taking third is—"

Adam and Luke whooped so loud, Kate missed the rest of it. And now Holly and Twiggy were jumping about, whooping louder than Adam. "We did it," they shrieked.

"Did what?"

"Third place, you idiot."

Kate opened her mouth, but no words came out. She shook her head, convinced she was dreaming. The announcer rattled off more names—Spruce Hill, Fox Meadow, and all the others—except for Stonewall Farm.

"What's going on?" Kate said.

Twiggy shrugged. "I guess they got eliminated."

"It happens," Luke said, leaning forward to touch Kate's shoulder. "So, about tomorrow night? Are you busy?"

"No," Holly said.

"Yes," Kate said.

Holly stepped on Kate's foot. "No, you're not."

"Good," Luke said, sounding relieved. "Because I've been conned into a Disney film with my sister—and her friends." He glanced toward the barn door where all three girls were now giggling and nudging one another. Then he dazzled Kate with a smile, and his eyes did that amazing crinkly thing again. "So, would you come with me, just to help out?"

"Yes," Holly said.

This time, Kate didn't argue.

Book 14, FAIR PLAY

With Princess Twiggy's help, Holly engineers a date between Kate and Luke Callahan, but her matchmaking plans turn sour when Luke tells Kate she needs a better horse.

About the Author

MAGGIE DANA'S FIRST RIDING LESSON, at the age of five, was less than wonderful. She hated it so much, she didn't try again for another three years. But all it took was the right horse and the right instructor and she was hooked.

After that, Maggie begged for her own pony and was lucky enough to get one. Smoky was a black New Forest pony who loved to eat vanilla pudding and drink tea, and he became her constant companion. Maggie even rode him to school one day and tethered him to the bicycle rack . . . but not for long because all the other kids wanted pony rides, much to their teachers' dismay.

Maggie and Smoky competed in Pony Club trials and won several ribbons. But mostly, they had fun—trail riding and hanging out with other horse-crazy girls. At horse camp, Maggie and her teammates spent one night sleeping in the barn, except they didn't get much sleep because the horses snored. The next morning, everyone was tired and cranky, especially when told to jump without stirrups.

Born and raised in England, Maggie now makes her home on the Connecticut shoreline. When not mucking stalls or grooming shaggy ponies, Maggie enjoys spending time with her family and writing the next book in her TIMBER RIDGE RIDERS series.

Sign up for our mailing list and be among the first to know when the next Timber Ridge Riders book will be out. Send your email address to:

timberridgeriders@gmail.com

For more information about the series, visit:
www.timberridgeriders.com

or check out our Facebook page:
www.facebook.com/TimberRidgeRiders

Note: all email addresses are kept strictly confidential.

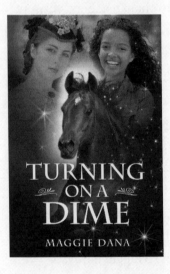

Two girls, two centuries apart, and the horse that brings them together

TURNING ON A DIME

This exciting time-travel adventure (with horses, of course) from the author of TIMBER RIDGE RIDERS is available in print and ebook from your favorite book store.

For information and to read an excerpt, visit:
www.maggiedana.com